She'd thought she was safe now, but apparently not...

Rosalind pulled out her room key then hesitated before she keyed the lock. Forehead resting against the door, she spoke without turning. "Where's your back up?"

He stood to her side and didn't pretend to misunderstand. "Up a couple of floors."

"Am I supposed to come to them once you've weaseled the truth out of me?"

"It's not like that, Roz."

She seemed to deflate, leaning against the door, as all the fight drained out of her. "No? Then what is it like, Ty? What the hell brought you halfway across the country in the middle of winter? You don't even like Florida."

"Well, for Christ's sake, you hate Florida."

"Who told you that?"

"You did."

"Oh, yeah, you're right."

Sighing, she slid her key through the lock then turned so she was looking in his direction while pushing open the door. As a result, the explosion grazed her back instead of hitting her square in the face.

Rosalind Summerton led a charmed existence, right up to the day she accepted an invitation to visit a family in the Middle East and learn more about the culture up close and personal. It became far too up close, and she barely escaped with her life. She no longer has faith in herself as a survivor, and she needs to stay somewhere that she can see miles in every direction. Cold would also be nice.

Tyler Randolph has lost faith in himself and his judgement of people, especially women, after his wife left, along with his truck, trailer, and horse. He's wondering why he's bothering. Until he meets his new tenant: tall, sexy, intriguing—and scared.

Can these two cautious people have enough faith to try one more time?

In *A Question of Faith* by Mona Karel, we return to Storm-haven, this time with Rosalind Summerton, who goes to the New Mexico ranch after a harrowing experience in the Middle East. While she thinks her ordeal is over and she just needs a quiet place to recuperate, she is soon proven wrong. She and Tyler Randolph, the owner of the ranch, get off on the wrong foot when Ty thinks she's a romance author, which he doesn't like because it reminds him of his ex-wife, who used to read them all the time. But Ty is a sucker for wounded spirits, and Roz soon earns his sympathy for what she has been through. But when she refuses to be a victim and shows not only a survival mentality, but a determined strength and character he doesn't expect her to have, she also earns his respect—and his love. Now all he has to do is keep her safe and protect her from the scum who are trying to recapture her to use for their own nefarious purposes. Karel really has a way with words, weaving a sexy romance into a "black ops" thriller. Her characters and their trials and tribulations are scarily realistic, making you fidget with tension while turning pages as fast as you can. ~ *Taylor Jones, Reviewer*

A Question of Faith by Mona Karel is the second in her electrifying new romantic thriller series, *Stormhaven Love Stories*. Stormhaven is just that—a haven against the storm of PTSD—a ranch in rural New Mexico where anyone suffering from post-traumatic stress syndrome can find sanctuary, much-needed peace and quiet, privacy, and sympathetic comrades. The usual refugees are combat veterans, who have seen too much death and destruction and need a place to de-stress. So Stormhaven's owner, Tyler Randolph, is a bit taken aback when Rosalind Summerton, a successful high-fashion model and author, rents a small cabin on the ranch. But as Ty soon learns, Roz is suffering from PTSD just as much as any soldier, having recently been rescued from being abducted and held as a hostage in the Middle East. Now the terrorists are after her, as well as elite "black ops" units, both of whom want to use her for their own purposes, which are hardly in her best interests. The bad guys want to use her as an example of "wicked American whores" and a patsy/scapegoat for their plot to kill innocent civilians. The good guys—if you can call them that—want answers Roz doesn't even have, and they don't care how much they harm her in the process of getting them. Roz and Ty clash at first, but as their relationship heats up, so does the danger. And Ty is determined to protect her from everything...even herself. *A Question of Faith* is an excellent, well-written sequel to *A Question of Honor*. I loved Roz! She was so strong yet so vulnerable, you just can't help rooting for her. As the plot revs up, along with Ty and Roz's relationship, you'll end up both cheering in triumph and screaming in dismay. It's not a book you can read without getting emotionally involved—one you will want to keep on your shelf to read again and again. ~ *Regan Murphy, Reviewer*

ACKNOWLEDGEMENTS

As always, to Lauri, Faith, Jack, and the other wonderful people at Black Opal Books, who had had faith in me when I didn't have faith in myself. Also to Molly Evans, who willingly answered questions about being locked in a stone room without water. Thanks to her, Rosalind survived.

A
Question
of
Faith

A Stormhaven Love Story

Mona Karel

A Black Opal Books Publication

GENRE: WESTERN ROMANCE/ROMANTIC SUSPENSE

This is a work of fiction. Names, places, characters and incidents are either the product of the author's imagination or are used fictitiously, and any resemblance to any actual persons, living or dead, businesses, organizations, events or locales is entirely coincidental. All trademarks, service marks, registered trademarks, and registered service marks are the property of their respective owners and are used herein for identification purposes only. The publisher does not have any control over or assume any responsibility for author or third-party websites or their contents.

A QUESTION OF FAITH ~ A Stormhaven Love Story
Copyright © 2016 by Mona Karel
Cover Design by Jackson Cover Designs
All cover art copyright © 2016
All Rights Reserved
Print ISBN: 978-1-626945-33-3

First Publication: OCTOBER 2016

Published by Black Opal Books **http://www.blackopalbooks.com**

DEDICATION

To Jami Gray,
who reminded me how much I love to write.

Mmmmm-WAH

Chapter 1

Whoever came up with the expression "cursing a blue streak" must have shared an early winter morning with cowboys. Certainly the good-natured grumbling could turn the air blue, though the day seemed cold enough to freeze words in mid-speech. Rosalind wondered if, like Paul Bunyan's story, the words would thaw, come spring, and shock someone walking near the barns.

She laughed at her whimsy, at the morning, at the freedom of standing in the snow under a lowering sky filled with billowing clouds edged in early dawn, with nothing blocking her vision for miles. For the moment, life was good.

The morning chill seeped through her new shearling

jacket, sending tendrils of cold under the hem to tickle her body. Big city winter gear wasn't up to this mountain weather, even when she tried to conserve heat by squatting on a tree stump. Under stiff jeans, goose bumps rose along her folded legs, and despite the heavy flannel of her shirt, her nipples were painfully taut. She reached up to run her fingers through familiar long, thick hair, only to encounter short, coarse strands flattened under a wool cap, and she took a quick breath, remembering why the color was somewhere around dark drab, instead of the normal rich mink brown, although these days she didn't look in the mirror long enough to remember. The lack of silky weight on her neck reminded her enough all by itself.

Memories threatened, but in this morning's clean open air she could ignore them. Only at night, trapped within walls shrouded in night's shadows, did she wish for the oblivion of amnesia. A coward's way out, perhaps. She'd proven to herself she was not the stuff of which heroes were made.

For now, in this place of open skies and cold air, she could push away those memories and enjoy the moment, watching cowboys prepare well bred horses for a day's work. Listening to them grumble good-naturedly, and filing away the cadence of their voices for possible future use. Since her arrival two days before at the secluded ranch in the mountains of northern New Mexico, the men had been polite but distant. They acknowledged her presence as a guest, returned her greetings, but didn't go out of their way to interfere with whatever she did. It was comforting to know she was accepted but wouldn't be bothered.

The walk-through barn door opened, and a new man joined the group. Physically he didn't seem much larger than most of the others, but his carriage and movement drew her eye. From the reaction of the gathered crew, turning their attention in his direction, it looked like the boss man was back from his trip. The group exchanged smiles and nods, then one of the cowboys pointed in her direction

The new man looked up the slope. Rosalind sank lower, automatically minimizing her height. They couldn't possibly see her sitting so still in the shadow of the trees. She felt her tension ease when the cowboys mounted then moved off after a final exchange of good-natured grousing, the horses streaming clouds through their nostrils like amiable dragons.

Unfortunately, the boss man was still coming her way. Perhaps the men who shared her arrival hadn't seen her, and he wasn't actually looking for her. Perhaps if she sat very still, he would walk on by and up to the charming old house on the hill. She recognized the memory of being hunted.

"Ms. Summerton?"

His voice was deep and smooth, like fine whiskey and old traditions. Laughter and years spent under the sun and wind left lines etched in his face, bracketing bright blue-green eyes. He removed his hat as he approached, revealing thick sun-gold hair. Merciful heavens, the man was a walking billboard for cowboys.

"I'm sorry I wasn't here to greet you when you first arrived. I'm Tyler Randolph. Welcome to Stormhaven." He removed the glove from his right hand and held it, plus his hat, in his left hand. Rosalind stood as she slid off her own glove to grasp his hand briefly. Large and calloused, strong, capable, and…warm. She felt the warmth easing into her skin and up her arm. She'd been cold for so very long.

"No problem, Mr. Randolph. Everyone has been most helpful, especially your housekeeper, and your ranch has more than met my requirements." She pulled her fingers back, missing the warmth of his hand.

His eyes were on a level with hers, though he stood downslope. Head tilted, he squinted a bit against the sun, as though he was trying to see her more clearly among the dark trees. How polite he was, pretending to want to get a closer look at her.

She knew he saw legs that were too long and thin. A body that bypassed slender and dove straight to gaunt. The mane of hair that once was her major attraction was gone, of course. The sad remnants were currently hidden under her knit cap. Her eyes hadn't changed, still that irritating purple that made people think she had the IQ of an eggplant.

Not that it mattered what he thought. Of course not.

His lips quirked in a smile it seemed he shared only with her. "Since I received your request through a third party, I'm curious, what were your requirements?"

"Some place cold and peaceful, with no hunting." Actually, she wanted somewhere as far away from the desert, guns, and death as she could get.

"You rented the cabin for six months, are you taking a long vacation from work?"

"Not really. I needed some time alone, and since I'm self-employed it doesn't matter where I work."

"What kind of work, if I can be nosy?"

"I write."

The private smile slipped away as if it had never been on his lips, and she felt the cold seep once again into her bones. "Oh? What do you write?"

"Whatever sells." Generally she didn't share this very personal part of her life, particularly not with someone she just met.

"I hear those romances sell." His voice could not have held more scorn.

"They certainly do," she said, not bothering to confirm or deny what she wrote. "So do thrillers, mysteries, and many end of the world by destruction books."

His well-shaped lips flattened into a smirk, and he swept one of those warm hands through his thick hair before settling the Western hat on his head, pulling it down as if for emphasis.

"At least those have some real content."

"Because they're written about death and destruction and the ugly side of life, instead of about hope and the belief in a possible happy future between two people?" She would not give him the satisfaction of rolling her eyes, but she couldn't stop the breath escaping from her lips.

There was no mistaking the sincerity in his expression. "Because they're about reality, not some fancied up nonsense glossed over with sex."

He was serious, whatever the reason for his opinion. "Yes, the world coming to an end tomorrow due to an asteroid or volcano or weather inversion is definitely reality. Not to mention a zombie apocalypse." Realizing if she continued, she was liable to say or do something she might come to regret, she took a deep breath and strove for a less aggressive tone. "Personally, there's too much reality in our world these days. We all deserve a nice dose of fantasy from time to time." She managed a smile, though she could feel her teeth grind. This sort of discussion hadn't bothered her for years. When had her habitual easy dialogue disappeared?

"Waste of time in my opinion," he muttered.

"It's obvious you aren't helping contribute to the financial needs of writers, Mr. Randolph." This time she managed a smile, one practiced enough to be wide and bright, despite the dull surrounding features that remained makeup free.

He stared at her, his mouth opening as if to respond, only to close slowly, no doubt wondering where that smile came from. He shook his head before tugging the brim of his hat, jamming it lower on his head. "Everyone's entitled to their own point of view, I guess."

"They certainly are." She watched him turn away and suddenly felt colder than ever.

⁊⁖⁊

Fresh snow squeaked under his boots as Ty strode uphill to his house, reaching for and not achieving the calm he usually found when returning to the ranch. What started out as a pleasant conversation with an attractive stranger had sure deteriorated fast. But knowing the person sharing his ranch for the next six months wrote the kind of books his worthless ex-wife had been addicted to didn't sit well with him. He tried to recall what Rosalind Summerton looked like without turning around. Her words, spoken softly as though her throat hurt, kept him from remembering much more than a wide mouth, odd-colored eyes, and hair hidden by a wool cap. She did seem awfully thin, probably one of those women who was afraid to gain an ounce, thinking her lunch buddies would make fun of her.

He stomped up the stone steps and out of the cold, letting the door slam behind him in a satisfactory manner.

"Take off your boots, Tyler Randolph, before you track up my floor," Maria, his diminutive housekeeper, called out from the kitchen. She liked doing floors least of any part of housework, but refused to give in. Once the floors were done, she was obsessive about keeping him off of them.

"I missed you too, Maria." He padded in stockinged feet to the cozy warmth of the big family kitchen, having left his outerwear in the front room. Enticing odors of all-day-long cooking wafted from the oven, along with the ambrosia of fresh-brewed coffee.

"You go on a trip, you come back." She shrugged, poured out a mug of coffee, and set it in front of him. "You want to be missed, get yourself a wife. I have better things to do."

He wrapped his hand around the hot coffee mug and took a deep, appreciative sip. "You're in a good mood this morning. Bad night on the town?"

She didn't respond to the jibe, turning back to the stove to check a boiling pot. She seldom left the ranch, except to shop. "My sister called yesterday. Her husband gets out of jail soon, and she's worried."

"He went in for abusing her, didn't he?" Ty sipped at his coffee, watching for her nod, and waited for more information. Maria continued working at the stove. "You know she's welcome to come out here and stay, if she wants."

"The children are doing well in school. It wouldn't be fair to change them now." She set a plate of pancakes and bacon in front of him, and went back to cleaning.

"Do you want me to send someone to help her?"

The offer was considered seriously before she shook her head. "No, it could make things worse right now. Maybe later. I might need to go there myself for a while, if that would be all right."

"I think I can avoid starving for a while. There's always frozen dinners." Usually that brought a scold. When she didn't offer her usual acerbic comment, he knew she was worried. "Whatever you need, let me know." Then, to distract her, "Have you met our new tenant?"

Now she did turn away from the stove, her expression lightening. "Miss Summerton? Of course. She's a lovely young woman, but so thin. I think she's been sick."

"She's a writer," he bit out, before he could control himself.

She smiled at his growl. "Everyone makes money somehow, Tyler."

"Well, as long as she stays out of my way."

Now she did frown at him. "Your mother raised you to have better manners than you're showing. That young woman has seen some bad times. The least you can do is try to be polite to her."

Taken aback by Maria's comment, Ty hesitated, staring at the shiny oil floating on top of his coffee. "What makes you think she's seen some bad times? Her clothes look new and not cheap, and she was able to rent the cottage for cash up front."

"Money isn't the only reason for bad times. You should know that."

"Not for ranchers," he shot back, ignoring the twinge of guilt as he almost agreed with Maria's chastisement. "At least not most of the ones I know."

"Well, she's kept to herself so far, but she seems careful to look around before she goes anywhere." She paused, the toast-colored skin on her brow pulling tight. "And her lights stay on most of the night."

"Maybe that's her writing schedule. You know she writes those romances like Lana used to read?"

Maria frowned, spoon held over the mixing bowl. "She told you that?"

"Yes—" He stopped and thought back through the brief exchange, before reluctantly admitting, "No, maybe not. Not sure now if she did tell me what she wrote."

"You might ask her again. Even if she does write romances, she writes books that make other people happy. What's wrong with that?" Maria continued mixing the batter. "You are usually tolerant."

"Well, Stormhaven needs the money from her rental, and it's not as though she's going to get in my way much."

An undignified snort sounded. "That will be difficult. She'll be eating dinner here tonight, and so will you." When she looked up, her smile seemed way too smug.

"Why's that?"

"I knew you'd be home tonight and you would want to have your guest come for dinner."

For a minute, Ty wondered if Maria was giving in to her occasional urge to matchmake, then he decided she was simply being nice to another lost soul. "I don't see where dinner will be much of a problem. She probably doesn't eat much anyway. What are we having?"

"I've made a pot roast with winter vegetables and we'll have biscuits and a salad."

"I guess the salad's for our guest?" He really tried to keep the disdain out of his voice.

"No, the salad's for me." Laced with humor, the answer came from a new voice behind him.

Ty spun around to see his best friend's wife in the entryway. "When did you get in, and where's Dev?"

"He's bringing in something from the car. We got in about an hour ago. We had a quick delivery from Phoenix to Denver, so we dropped back down when we were done." She said this all in a rush as she deposited her scarf, gloves and coat on a chair, then ruffled her short hair.

Ty enveloped her in an embrace, wondering once again at how short she was—her personality always made her seem much larger—and at how lucky his best friend was to find this woman.

"You manhandling my wife, Randolph?" Speak of the devil. Devin stepped in and leaned a shoulder against the doorjamb.

Ty grinned, but didn't let go of the female in his arms. "Just thinking about what I might need to do to take her away from your sorry self."

Sydney pushed him away with an indelicate snort. "Looks like I got here in time to save you from degenerating into a narrow-minded, right-leaning bigot, you old rancher you."

Feigning taking a hit, he clamped a hand to his chest and stumbled back a step or two. "See what happens when you're not around to keep me in line?"

"We have someone else around now who can maybe teach Tyler to have more respect for women with spine," Maria called out from the kitchen.

Curiosity sharpened Sydney's attention. "Oh, what's this?"

Hoping to nip whatever hare-brained ideas were floating around inside Sydney's skull, he explained, "I took a six month rental on the cottage through our agent. Didn't know at the time it was a woman. Turns out she's a writer."

Excitement lit her face. "Wonder if I've read any of her work?"

"Doubt it, she writes those romances," Ty said.

The smile breaking across her face was filled with mischief. "You think I don't read romance?"

Folding his arms across his chest, Ty shot back, "Thought you'd be more of the war lord/soldier of fortune type reader."

She wrinkled her nose. "Why would I want to read about shooting people and crawling through the jungle? I lived through enough of that myself." Though it was said with a laugh, there was a grim note in her voice. Before Ty could apologize, she shook her head and gave him a small smile.

"So, you're saying you read romances because you don't get enough romance in your life?" Devin's deep voice rumbled through the room and his hard face softened into a rare smile.

She shrugged, her gaze bright. "Well, no one's brought me flowers or carried me through a crowd of cheering peasants lately."

Before she could continue, he swept over and lifted her in his arms, twirling her around until she shrieked with laughter. The trio moved into the kitchen.

"Enough, be careful of the walls!" Maria warned, eyeing the couple. "I don't know if you two are a good influence on Tyler anymore."

They laughed. Devin let his wife slide down to the floor, then turned to Ty. "So, hanging good?"

"'Bout the same. You?"

"Can't complain. Been in the damned city too much but other than that, holding up okay."

"You here for long this trip?"

"Depends on if we get a call. For now, we're just hanging out. Syd's gotta check in later." He headed to the counter where Maria set out another cup of coffee. "So, you have a guest?"

"Someone rented the cabin for six months. Sorry, old man, thought you'd be gone for a while."

Devin brought the cup up and indulged before responding. "No prob. Takes too long to warm up if we're only going to be around for a couple days. Who's the tenant?"

Ty blew out a breath. "You'll get to meet her. Maria's invited her to dinner."

౿౩౿౩

The sun eased behind the mountains, lengthening the shadows as Rosalind prepared for dinner with her landlord. A short nap helped restore some energy but it generally took being outside, facing the wide expanse of snow covered plains with no visual obstruction, before she was able to breathe normally. Set among pine trees, the cabin was charming and private, but none of the windows were very large, and most faced the pine trees or the mountain, giving her the sensation of being closed in.

Being outside as much as possible was helping, as well as using the daylight for sleep. Since sleeping all night was still impossible, she spent that time losing herself in her writing, lights blazing to hold the dark at bay. She promised her future self many hours of sleep in a dark room with covers pulled to her chin. Another issue to lay at the door of her own foolishness. For now, she drew in a deep breath of open air and readied herself for a brisk walk.

Multiple layers protected her body from the crisp cold air: silk long underwear, flannel-lined jeans, a wool sweater, and her shearling jacket. A wool scarf covered her hair and a woolen hat on top of that held in the warmth. A hood might be more efficient, but hoods blocked too much of her vision. Her feet were covered by silk socks, then thick wool, and stuffed into fur lined boots. She was ready to head up to the house.

Someone had shoveled a path between her cabin and the other buildings. Grateful, she made a mental note to find out who to thank, as she stepped back inside long enough to pick up a powerful flashlight for the walk back.

Sounds of disturbance drew her along the path. A small woman, well bundled, dashed into an open area, closely followed by a larger male, clad only in a flannel shirt, jeans, boots, and a cowboy hat. He closed the distance between them quickly. As he reached out to grab the woman, she dropped as if she had tripped. Then Rosalind watched the man flying through the air, turning neatly to land on his knees in a snow bank.

The woman immediately pounced and what Rosalind initially assumed were sounds of fright turned out to be hysterical laughter as the woman shoved handfuls of snow down the man's neck.

Pulling back quietly, Rosalind decided to leave what was about to become an intimate scene when both bodies stilled, and their heads turned simultaneously in her direction.

The couple stood, the man using his hat to brush snow from his legs. The woman studied her with a small, polite smile. "Hello, you must be Rosalind. We were coming down to escort you to dinner."

"Ha!" The man bumped the small woman with his hip but she slid away before it could have any impact. "You were trying to sneak out and meet her before I could so you could have girly-girl talk."

Rosalind could only gape, speechless, while trying to bring her skittering emotions under control. The smaller woman hesitated then stepped forward alone, lightly touching the large man's hand as she did so. "I'm Sydney." She hesitated, glanced over her shoulder with an impish grin. "Sydney Starke."

Rosalind thought she heard a grumbled "Damned right, you are" but considering the man wore a slight smile and his gaze held a proprietary glint, it seemed more of a fake complaint.

"My glowering over-protective husband, Devin," Sydney offered.

Rosalind nodded but did not step forward. "Rosalind Summerton, but you obviously know that already." She extended her hand, then smiled when their clasp was more a matter of thick gloves than joined fingers.

Sydney peered closely into the shade cast by Rosalind's hat. "Are you all right?"

Rosalind tensed then offered her brightest smile. "Never better. I think the air here is more restoring than good champagne."

From the expression on the small woman's face, she obviously wasn't as convincing as she'd hoped. "I know, we miss it when we have to go to a city." Sydney stepped to the side, waving Rosalind forward.

They started up to the house together and Rosalind decided to make small talk. "Do you go to cities often?"

"That all depends on where the jobs take us. We work free-lance and sometimes end up in a city."

Remembering the concrete canyons of the city closing in on her, Rosalind muttered, "This is so much more beautiful."

"Yeah, it's rough to leave but great to get back. We're hoping to build our own place here soon, further away from the main part of the ranch. Devin used to live in the cabin you're renting." She glanced across to her husband and shared a small smile.

"I'm sorry—"

Sydney waved her hand. "Not to worry, we're here so rarely, you're more than welcome to stay."

They came into the house and began removing layers. Uncovered, Sydney was even smaller than Rosalind had thought, but her body displayed a toughness under the soft rose colored sweater.

Gloves came off, revealing a spectacular set of nails.

Catching the direction of Rosalind's gaze, Syd held her hand up, showing them off with a comic flair. "Yeah, it's my one real indulgence. Gotta keep the fingers decorated."

Rosalind kept her own hands curled, not wanting to reveal the still healing nailbeds and ragged quicks earned when she tried to dig her way out of a stone cell.

As the wrappings transferred from bodies to convenient resting places, Sydney's eyes narrowed as she took a closer look at Rosalind. "Somehow I think we've met before."

Rosalind shrugged, half turning away while she attempted to fluff her hair. "Anything is possible. I've been a lot of places."

"Not sure if we've met in person or…something. You look familiar."

"Maybe you saw her on the back of a book?" Tyler strolled into the room, hands in the pockets of his Western-cut slacks. "She writes and must be successful to afford the rent on that cottage."

Silence fell with a heavy weight. Devin turned his head abruptly, brows gathering in a frown. Mouth pressed in a straight line, Tyler seemed embarrassed by his tone as well as his words, but he plunged on. "Nothing wrong with writing books. Too bad some books give people false ideas."

"Like people meeting and building lives?" Rosalind shot back.

"Like happily ever after. It doesn't exist."

"Umm, Ty?" Sydney glanced over at Devin and back, with a slight smile softening the determined lines on her face.

Tyler flipped one large hand in the air. "You guys are still on your honeymoon."

"And will be for the next forty or so years." Devin held out a glass of whiskey to his friend and partner. "Anyone else?"

Sydney took a glass of wine, Rosalind shook her head then sucked in a deep breath. "What is your real problem with romance books?"

Sydney and Devin drew a collective gasp.

"My wife read romance books, Ms. Summerton. She used them as her escape from the reality of being the wife of a working rancher. When she left, she took my truck, my trailer, and my prize stallion. She left her books behind."

Rosalind hesitated, searching for the rest of the story. Ty's voice was cold but a sense of loss, of failure, emanated from the large rancher. "She was a dedicated reader, and she left her books behind?"

"Made for a really great fire that winter, warmed me more than she ever did."

Rosalind frowned and noticed the other two avoided her gaze, but Sydney seemed pensive. Then she tipped her wine glass up to her mouth, finishing the dark red liquid. "Lana is my sister," she said. "Fortunately Ty lets me visit, especially since I brought back said truck, trailer, and stallion."

Ty finally had the grace to blush and set down his untouched drink. "Sorry to unload on you like that. You'll think Western hospitality is as much a fairy tale as romance books."

As an apology, it left much to be desired, but Rosalind decided to let it slide for now. There was obviously a lot more to the issue than a reader marrying a non-reader.

ᘓᕽᘖ

"Summer!" Sydney said, sitting straighter and staring directly into Rosalind's eyes.

Rosalind stilled, contemplating the bite of delicious stew on her spoon. So good, but she was already full. Welcoming the distraction, she smiled tightly.

Devin snorted and leaned over to contemplate his wife's expression. "No, Syd, it's snowing outside. Snow means winter."

"You have to sleep sometime, big boy." Syd turned back to Rosalind. "I'm right, aren't I?"

Cornered, Rosalind nodded then waited for what invariably came next—how different she looked, what happened, where had she been? Syd turned to the men. "I had a job, the daughter wanted to be a model. By the time I was done, I knew all the major players in the industry." She turned back to Rosalind. "The cameras love you."

Rosalind took a deep breath. What were the odds of someone on a remote New Mexico ranch recognizing her? "The cameras love anyone with a touch of Marfan syndrome, which elongates my bones, and an overactive metabolism. I was lucky to be in the right place at the right time and know some really good photographers."

Ty stared, brow furrowed.

"You haven't done much lately," Sydney said.

"It's been a while since I did much fashion modeling. Some book covers for a friend, but that's all." She decided she could not force down another bite, at least not around the lump forming in her stomach. "I was overseas for a while."

She noticed intense looks between the three of them. This might be one group where overseas had an entirely different meaning than for most of the people she knew.

e⁄oe⁄o

Sydney let herself back into the house, stomping snow off her boots then toeing them off and dropping her jacket on a chair before padding into the living room. The fire had died down to glowing coals, barely illuminating Devin and Ty sitting back in the deep cushioned chairs with glasses of brandy at their elbows.

"Well, that was quick." Devin's voice rumbled from

where he sat in the deep chair, face in the shadows, legs extended to the fire.

Sydney perched on the arm of Devin's chair, reaching for his brandy snifter. "She doesn't dawdle, that's for sure."

"Those long legs are for more than just looks?" Devin's deep voice rumbled.

"Keep it up, big guy."

"Just making an observation." He took back the brandy, set it on the side table, and pulled her into his lap. After a token protest, she settled but didn't relax.

"What's got you frowning?" Ty asked, leaning forward.

"Remember when Powers wanted me to work for him?"

Both men nodded.

"It was an extraction. Extremely sensitive and hush hush. Somewhere in the Middle East, one of those small countries we don't hear much about. Seems a former model got herself kidnapped but no one would admit she'd even been there."

Ty straightened. "What are you saying?"

"I need more information first, but I'm thinking there might be more to your guest than you realize." She snuggled closer to Devin, needing the comfort of his arms, not saying anything more.

Chapter 2

A dark ribbon rolled down the mountain, slowly evolving into a herd of milling cattle and attendant cowboy outriders. Near a stand of trees, Rosalind watched from her perch on a rock in the sun. She leaned back against the stone surface as the herd drew closer and picked out the various shades of red or brown on the cattle moving alongside the equine hides ranging from solid to spotted. Finally, she focused on the individual outriders and herdsmen. From here, she could identify them by name and recall shared conversations, some of which would no doubt find a home in a future book. Part of her attention remained on the scene in front of her, while she allocated the rest to the small phone pressed to her ear.

"Tell me again why you thought you had to leave New York for some foreign country." Despite the physical space and the remote location of the ranch, the voice was so clear she could almost hear traffic noises on the other end.

"Try clear skies, no horns honking, fresh air, nice people." *Not having to look over your shoulder at every loud noise, being able to walk alone at night without fear,* she continued mentally. "And, smart boy, New Mexico happens to be part of the United States. Sits between Arizona and Texas, right below Colorado."

"Aspen?"

"Several hours north."

"But what are you *doing* there?"

Regaining my sanity, she thought, and lifted her face to the sky, reveling in the sunlight. The weather had warmed to a balmy forty degrees and she was only wearing one pair of socks with her fleece lined boots. Squawking in her ear brought her back to the conversation.

"Getting more work done than any other three-week stint in the last few years."

"That's good for you but when are you coming back? I need my favorite model."

"Trust me, you don't. You remember what I look like, I'm hardly a fairy queen anymore."

"True, but I have a commission for a different line of covers, more of a warrior princess, and I think you'd be perfect. Especially as much as you've been working out."

That was true. Once she left of the hospital, she'd followed through on her vow to never again be at the mercy of someone else because she had no idea how to defend herself. The result wasn't a lot more bulk, but she did have a new muscle definition and a modicum more confidence.

"I'll be here a while yet. Why don't you come out?"

There was no way to describe the noises emanating from her cell phone and she felt her mouth moving in a wide smile. "I can't be somewhere without a Starbucks or a decent spa."

Trust Tony to make her laugh even when she didn't think she ever would again. "Toughen up, city boy. There's a Starbucks in Trinidad."

"Well, of course there is, but if you were in Trinidad, I'd be there with you looking at all the cabana boys."

"Trinidad, Colorado, goof. It's maybe seventy-five miles away, so popping out for a gingerbread latte might be a bit problematic."

"You very funny girl. Tell me, what is there to do all day?"

"Lest you forget, I do write books sometimes."

"Even you can't write twenty-four-seven. As a matter of fact, it doesn't sound like you're writing now. It sounds like you're outside."

"You noticed. Well, right now I'm watching a herd of cattle being moved from one mountain pasture to another by four or five cowboys on horses."

"Cowboys? You didn't tell me there were cowboys."

"It's a ranch, what else would be here? Chinchillas?"

"Are they cute?"

"Chinchillas?"

"Cowboys." His voice was starting to show impatience.

She smirked, but since he couldn't see it...

"Some of them, but I'm fairly sure none of them want to act out *Brokeback Mountain* with you."

"As if." And she could picture his eyes rolling. "Happens I've been looking for some scenes for a layout of Western icons."

"You haven't seen anything Western until you've seen a horse and rider silhouetted against the setting sun, coming back from a long day's work. Hard to say which one is more tired, both kind of slouch down the mountain."

"Okay, I'm there. Can you pick me up in that Albaturkey place?"

"Albuquerque, you ignorant city boy. Try Denver, it's actually closer, and has more flights."

"You better be taking care of your skin so I can get some close up shots of you too, barbarian princess."

"Yeah, yeah, yeah." She leaned back, cradling the phone against her shoulder while she opened another button on her jacket. Without the near constant wind, it was almost warm. "You be sure to dress warm and pack your boots." After spending a few more minutes making plans, she ended the call, feeling somehow lighter than she had for a while.

She went back to watching the workers, refusing to let herself admit she was looking for one person in particular, a bit taller, a bit wider in the shoulders, on a cantankerous gray stallion. He'd been back from his latest trip for a week but she hadn't actually seen him. She looked toward the barn, spotting the gray stallion in an outside pen and wondered if, unlike his rider, he would welcome new friends. Only one way to find out.

⁐ᗡᥱᗡ⁐

"So, you're the infamous Mosby."

The gray stallion stood hipshot, eyes half closed. He swiveled one lazy ear in her direction when she moved closer to the pen. She stopped a respectful distance from the metal bars in case his relaxed stance was a ruse.

"That's the one. Watch your fingers, Sydney spoiled him something fierce while she had him."

The warning came from the barn entrance, a thread of humor in the deep voice. She didn't need to look around to identify the speaker, the vibration in her bones let her know. "She didn't seem like a horse person."

"She wasn't. When my ex-wife left, she took Mosby with her. After she got tired of punishing me for marrying her, she called Sydney to clean up her mess. While we were waiting for all the pieces to fall into place, Sydney learned how to take care of him, then rented a place where she could keep him in the backyard. Seems the cranky old fart couldn't stand being cooped up in a stall and needed open spaces all around him."

She didn't turn around to look, in case he could see how much she agreed with needing open spaces. "Pretty brave, taking on something like that without knowing what you're getting into."

"That's Syd for you. Best thing to ever happen to Dev, that's for sure." Ty's voice came closer, along with the soft thud of his boots on the cleared ground. She felt the heat of his body against her back and turned to find him standing almost too close.

"Actually, I meant your ex-wife. You said she was a city girl and never really took to ranch life?"

"For some reason she thought 'outside Santa Fe' was ten minutes, not two hundred miles." He studied her, blue-green eyes glittering from under his hat brim, an arrested expression on his face. "I always did kind of wonder how she pulled it off, but when Lana wanted to get something done, she always managed somehow."

A dark velvety nose pushed between them, and Mosby nudged at Ty's pocket. His scowl didn't convince the horse or Rosalind. "You worthless flea bag," he said, "you think everyone has treats for you. I should turn you loose in the mountains, let you fend for yourself."

Rosalind reached into her back pocket and pulled out

a large carrot. "Is this what you're looking for, you silly old horse?"

Mosby turned from Ty, nosing the treat in her hand before biting off the end and working the carrot in his mouth to his back teeth where he crunched away, his ears tipping sideways as if listening to the hollow sound of carrot being ground between back teeth.

"Now you look like some common mule." Ty kept the false gruffness in his voice. The stallion ignored him and reached for the rest of the carrot, then lowered his head for some scratching between his eyes. "Doesn't seem you're much of a stranger to horses."

"Not hardly. Mom was horse crazy and took every job she could that had to do with horses. That's where my name came from—Rosalind."

He frowned as if she had presented him with a complex navigation question.

Taking pity on him, she explained, "Rosalind was a Standardbred mare, very famous. Mom named me after her. She told people it was from Shakespeare, but it was from the horse. The only Shakespeare she ever read was *As You Like It*, after people started asking her about the play. Otherwise she read about horses."

"Would she like to come out here? We could sure use more horse crazy people."

"Lost her about five years ago. Cancer."

"Sorry."

The sympathy seemed genuine and she managed a

nod. “She had a great life. I do have someone coming to visit—a photographer. He’s used me as a model before. I’ll be picking him up in Denver in a couple days.”

An odd expression crossed Ty’s face. Irritation? Certainly not jealousy.

“Happens I need to go up to Denver soon, want some company?”

She glanced at him sideways, wondering where this sudden geniality came from. “Sure, why not? I’ll even let you drive.

As it turned out, Rosalind ended up alone at the Denver airport, searching for Tony in a swarm of arriving passengers. At least his hair was blond instead of the bright fuchsia it was last time she saw him. Of course, the blond was a rather improbable shade of bright against his dark skin, but at least it was semi believable. Unlike the Madison Avenue cowboy outfit he was wearing.

“Where did you get those boots, city boy?”

Tony raised his leg to show off the offending footwear, heavily decorated with etched scrolling and higher than normal heels. The exiting passengers separated to go around them, and Rosalind pulled him out of the main stream.

“Aren’t they the gas? There’s a new Western-wear store near my apartment. We all went out gang shopping last night.”

"Not to be confused with other gang activity? Well, you might find they're a little hard to keep clean. And unless you have something heavier than that leather coat and fancy shirt, we need to do some serious shopping. You're going out where the snow piles almost as high as the manure."

Tony grinned, his mahogany skin stretching into deep wrinkles. "As long as the horses are noble and the cowboys are handsome, the rest I can deal with just fine."

ଔଔଔ

Ty checked his watch and shifted in the saddle, trying to see a little farther down the road.

"Relax, boss," Jamie said, obviously resisting a smirk. "Even if she left Denver right after breakfast she won't get here much before lunch."

Ty blew out a breath and heeled Mosby up the next hill. "No idea when she'll get here, she didn't leave much of a message."

And why in the world hadn't she waited for him? He said he'd take her to Denver. She could have waited a few more hours. Then maybe she could have returned the same day instead of staying overnight. Just like a woman not to wait for someone who had work to do.

ଔଔଔ

Rosalind eased her Envoy up to the cabin's front

door, drawing a deep breath and rolling her head on her neck as she turned off the ignition.

"When you said piled snow, you weren't exaggerating." Tony opened the door to step out only to slam it shut and stay inside the car. "Baby, it's *cold* out there."

"Now do you see why I made you buy all those useless clothes?"

"Why didn't you make me put them all on at once?"

Laughing, she opened her own door, then left it open to chill down the cozy interior. Tony's muttered complaints never quite expanded to outright threats, and he quickly followed when she opened the back hatch to pull out the luggage and shopping bags.

"Give me those, girl, you shouldn't be carrying."

"For pity's sake, I'm not a sissy. The day I can't outwork you, city boy, is a long ways away."

A long arm reached around her and grasped the handle of Tony's large leather suitcase. She was shouldered gently aside as Ty reached for the heavy camera bag. "You can get the shopping bags, I know better than to get between a woman and her goodies."

Tony gaped, then his dark brown eyes cut to hers and widened. Not speaking, Rosalind picked up her purse and some of the shopping bags then closed the vehicle after Tony picked up the rest.

They followed Ty quietly up the shoveled walkway to the front door.

To her surprise, the cabin was toasty warm. She'd

been afraid it would have chilled since she was away longer than planned.

"You really don't need to carry my bags," Tony protested mildly. "I could have managed even without Xena here's help."

"We try to treat guests well at Stormhaven." Ty's deep rumble seemed pleasant but Rosalind sensed an undercurrent of anger. Displeasure. Pissed off. "Sometimes they give us a hard time about it, but we do the best we can."

What the heck was that supposed to mean? Rosalind dropped her purse on the table inside the door, then turned left toward the extra room.

"I'll drop your bags in here, so you can put things away at your leisure."

Tony moved closer to Rosalind, still watching Ty. "Does he always glower like that?"

"Seems like."

Ty cocked his head, as if he had heard their low exchange, then set down the suitcases and stepped back. "Maria's planning some kind of stew for lunch, whenever you feel hungry. She wants to be sure to meet your new friend before she has to leave." He tipped one finger to his hat brim then strode out. The front door closed firmly behind him.

"Never thought I'd see the Marlboro Man up close and personal."

"Still haven't. Ty doesn't smoke. Told me he likes his lungs pink, same as his steak."

"Isn't that a charming image? Okay, girlfriend, spill."

Rosalind upended the shopping bag and started folding sweaters. "Don't know what you're talking about."

"Stop that." He batted her hands away from the sweater. "You know you've never been able to fold anything properly. Tell me about tall, dark, and glowering."

"He owns the ranch, divorced, hates romance writers."

"That shouldn't bother you." He stopped folding, turned to her, and narrowed his eyes. "Oh, no, you did not. Girl, you just love to sabotage yourself, don't you?"

"Can't think what you're talking about."

"You didn't tell him you write romance?"

"Nope. Just didn't tell him I *don't* write romance." Her smile was pure mischief, and Tony groaned.

"I guess it can't be any worse than pissing off Natasha."

Her smile widened, remembering. "Pinnacle of my career, I'd say."

"If your career was mischief making and irritation."

"We all go with our strengths."

⧼⧽

"The contract I have is for scenery at a working

ranch, preferably one that hasn't changed physically since it was first started. No problem with upgrading or modernizing the actual work areas, but they want a rustic look, side-by-side with the modern." Tony reached out for another biscuit to shamelessly sop up the soup juices. "Wonderful food."

"Our own beef, and Maria's good cooking. I just follow the re-heating instructions." Ty served himself more stew. "She asked me to apologize for not being here. She needed to pick up extra groceries for when she's away."

"Nice to know I'll be getting some decent meals. I was afraid I'd either have to fend for myself or suffer through another bout of 'Rosalind stomach.'"

"Unfair." Rosalind's tone was mild. "You got sick on the moldy cheese you insisted on adding to the pasta."

"Oh yeah, you're right." He watched her eating methodically for a minute. "Good to see you eat again. You might have put on a whole pound."

"Seven, jackass. Not that it's any of your business."

"You know your shape is always my business."

Ty looked back and forth between them as if following their banter. "I thought models were supposed to be thin."

"Not cadaverous. And Summer—her stage name—was never one of those extreme shapes even when she was in the business. Which she's not anymore, are you?"

"I doubt Ty is interested in what kind of modeling I did."

Before Ty could speak up, Tony forged ahead. "Wouldn't matter, you won't be doing that again for a while. For one thing, you need hair."

"Always so supportive, darling." Rosalind refused to let either of them see her discomfort.

Tony smirked but let the issue lie.

છ৩છ৩

Rosalind took up her position again, arching her back and lifting both arms above her head, sword in one hand and shield in the other. She was wearing the short, floaty sort of goddess dress that showed up on fantasy book covers, even though it made no sense on a woman who rode war horses and carried sharp pointy objects.

"Angle that shield just a bit more, you've got a shadow. No, the other direction. Good, hold it. Now twist a little to your right, drop the shield arm down, look over your shoulder. Look fierce. Not that fierce, you look like someone stole your parking place."

"Can we cut the chatter and be done? You may not have noticed, but it's cold out here and this dress is not meant for warmth."

"No worries, I can airbrush out those goose bumps, and the nipples will help sell the book." Humming, he changed lenses while studying her, then looking around at the light. "Okay, one foot up on the rock there, twist your hips. I want to get your face in a shadow but with a touch of light on your eyes."

Ty watched from behind the slender photographer, keeping himself in the shadow of the trees. They'd been at this for hours, generally in good humor but at times testy with each other. Using a wide collection of cameras Tony photographed Rosalind against trees, rocks, and the wide New Mexico sky.

While heading down to the barn that morning to check on a sick horse, Ty spotted them setting out in the pre-dawn and followed. Now it was time for him to head back to the house, and they were still working.

Despite the chill, the scene projected warmth and strength. From the tension in her body, Ty could read the story of a warrior queen ready to take on all comers. Her limbs were long and lean, with a strong muscle definition, without losing any femininity.

Rosalind tilted her head a degree more and must have seen him out of the corner of her eye. Her body went from supple to rigid, though she didn't move an inch.

Tony raised his head immediately and looked in the same direction, then sighed. "Take five, get warmed up."

Putting down her sword, Rosalind immediately grabbed a long cloak that lay aside outside the frame of the shot. She pulled it on with a minimum of fuss, slipping her arms through the slashes, turning away as she did up the buttons.

"Didn't mean to interrupt. Maria will have a big breakfast ready by now, or whenever you're finished."

"We need to get this done, Tony's got to leave tomorrow for his next shoot."

"I'm about as done as we can get with these backgrounds." He began packing up his cameras.

"What other backgrounds would you need?" Ty asked while not looking at Rosalind.

"Preferably some place that's not colder than a witch's left mammary. I love the natural light, but the snow glares in the middle of the day."

"Why not take a trip over to Phoenix? You could get some desert shots there."

The sword clattered against a rock, the sound breaking the morning peace. Rosalind bent over to pick it up, her normal grace absent.

Tony continued packing his gear. "That wouldn't be the kind of light I need, and besides who wants to keep mopping up sweat? We got some really good shots here, I should be able to make something of it. It's mostly for reference anyway."

Ty looked over, frowning at the photographer's words.

Tony zipped up another camera bag. "I generally use the actual photos as a reference for book covers. I had a lot of stock photos of nature girl here with longer hair, but that was a completely different look and none of it worked for this new series of books."

❦❦❦

"What kind of book covers?" Ty asked, reaching for another biscuit as they sat in the warmth of the kitchen.

"This current set is for a warrior priestess on some obscure planet out beyond the Milky Way. Some of the artwork goes into general fantasy stock. The old artwork was for a fairy queen/princess, ethereal creature. All long hair and billowing robes. Took a lot of those in the studio with fans blowing all over the place."

"But no studio for these?"

This time Rosalind didn't quite drop her fork, but it rattled hard against the plate when she set it down, then reached for her water glass. She sipped slowly, letting the water trickle down her suddenly dry throat while she fought for composure.

Thank God for Tony, who went blithely on while buttering another biscuit. "Not for these. Besides the studio is back in New York and Roz is out here. We got some fabulous shots out in the wilderness yesterday, and some of your hands working cattle, which will help with another book I'm working on about the anachronism and necessity of ranching. I bet you were born to it." Tony's expression held nothing but polite interest.

The subtle redirection gave Rosalind time to compose herself and try to fork down a few more mouthfuls of the fluffy scrambled eggs with cheese and peppers.

Maria brought in a fresh basket of biscuits and

stroked Rosalind's arm as she set the fragrant bowl in the middle of the table. "I made extra biscuits and put them in the freezer, Ty. You'll have enough for your breakfast or with the stew that's also in the freezer. I need to finish packing."

"What time do you need me to take you in the morning?" Ty asked.

"Don't be silly. I can drive myself. It's not that far to the airport, and the long term parking is not very expensive."

"Far enough to worry about you. What time's your flight?" he persisted.

"Just before noon."

"Hey, same as mine," Tony piped up. "If I can grab a ride with you two, Roz can catch up on her edits. Her editor's starting to call me since Roz somehow didn't leave the number here, and she's not always good about answering her cell."

Rosalind sat upright in her chair but the damage was done before she could open her mouth. She could only hope Tony would continue to protect her privacy while in the truck for so many hours with the inquisitive rancher.

Chapter 3

As usual when Ty returned to the ranch, he checked in first at the main barn. He trusted his staff, but he'd learned long ago there were times when being able to speak face to face made all the difference.

New fallen snow had been cleared away from paths. Jamie was waiting for him in the break room and offered a mug of coffee.

Ty hesitated before taking the mug. "Who made this pot, and when?"

"Ben did when you called from Raton."

Ty nodded, took the mug and a cautious sip. He nodded again and gulped.

"Ya know, boss, you're kind of a coffee snob."

"Yep. What's the good of having your own spread if you can't have decent coffee?"

Jamie thought about this for a minute then nodded his head. "Might have to let Davis go, or find something he can do away from the stock."

"Why's that?"

"He was roughing up that new mare you got, the sorrel? Trying to push her when she wasn't ready."

Ty was careful to set down the mug without breaking it. "Damn, that's a nice mare. I didn't want her ruined."

"She's not. Damnedest thing, your guest stepped in, cool as could be, told him to leave the mare alone. He mouthed off at her then challenged her to do better."

"And she did?" Ty kept his automatic desire to pound Davis into the dirt in check.

"You betcha. She had that half-wild mare docile as a hand-raised filly in under five minutes. First, she pulled off the big saddle, found a burr in the blanket. Then she put on one of the bareback pads she used when she was riding around the ranch with that yellow haired friend of hers.

"She hopped on the pole fence for an easy mount. Even with a storm coming down off the mountains, she had that mare stepping out on a loose rein faster than I've ever seen any of those coaches who charge a bundle for seminars."

"And Davis?"

"Kept mouthing off how he'd gotten her started,

how—" He hesitated, glancing at Ty from the corner of his eye.

"Might as well spit it all out."

"Stupid bullshit about a woman's place in the world."

"Is he still on the ranch?"

Relief crossed Jamie's face. "No sir, I told him he'd better not be here when you got in. Someone'd get his last pay to him."

Ty clapped a hand on Jamie's shoulder then turned toward the door. "Good call. It's bad enough he could have ruined a valuable horse. But no one acts that way toward a woman or a guest on this ranch." He hesitated, frowning. "Anyone else see?"

"Couple of the new hands. Seems like they weren't too sure what was acceptable here."

Ty reached for his coffee mug, to set it in the sink. "We'll need to make it very clear to them."

"Yes, sir. The rest were in with the counselor or not back from checking fences."

"Was this a regular day for the counselor?" Ty tried to recall the counseling schedule for the PTSD veterans he welcomed on his ranch.

"Not really. He's still making extra trips since Charlie…"

They eased out the barn door into the biting wind, reluctant to discuss the man who couldn't quite come all the way back to civilization and sacrificed himself to help

Sydney. Jamie took a deep, cleansing breath. "This new counselor seems to be doing a great job getting everyone to open up. When it looked like we'd get some nasty thunder with this last storm, he decided to come out."

"That's good to hear. I hope he lasts a while. Not all of them can relate to our crew so well."

"That's for sure. Kinda like not everyone can deal with a wall-eyed filly that needs a soft hand."

"Looks like we owe our guest some kind of thank you gift."

"Ya know?" Jamie looked up the hill to where the small cabin was partially concealed by large pine trees. "I haven't seen much of her since she put the mare up."

❧❧❧

Ty had never seen the cabin dark at night, and it was as close to night as it could be, with the setting sun stealing light from the ranch. He knew Rosalind was cautious of closed in, dark, places, though she had yet to share why. He wanted to know, same as he wanted to know a lot of things about his tenant.

He eased out of the SUV, noting the downed branches in the surrounding trees. Must have been one hell of a storm. The door wasn't latched, and he eased it open, listening. At first he heard nothing except the hum of the refrigerator. Then came a slight in-drawn breath, close to a sob.

He moved cautiously, knowing all too well how a careless noise could trigger problematic reactions.

❦

Backed into the corner of the room, Roz pulled herself into a tighter ball. Lightning and thunder crashed like mortar attacks, before going quiet. Too quiet. And it was cold, the way the desert got at night after daytime triple digits baked your skin and seared your eyes. On one level, she knew she was no longer in that tiny dark room in the stifling desert heat, but on another level she was afraid her mind was playing tricks on her, and she'd never really left.

There'd been the shooting, or was that thunder? She couldn't be sure so she stayed in the corner of the stone room, while the battle…or the wind?…raged around her. She smelled the dry dusty heat, felt the intense cold of a desert night settle into her bones. Soldiers had called for Ms. Summerton, they should have known her name was—

"Roz?" The deep voice, one she knew didn't belong here, slid through the cold. Not here, where death struck without warning.

A click, then a soft light filtered behind her covered eyes. "Come on, honey. Roz, come on, you're safe."

❦

Ty found her crouched in a corner under a soft wool throw, whimpering quietly as if she didn't want anyone to hear. He reached out to the closest lamp and turned it on. Her long fingers clutched at the edges of the throw, and he noticed the torn nails, the scarring. Sydney's nails looked like that under her fancy fakes. Why didn't Roz— he shook his head and brought himself back to the present need. Remembering advice from the counselors, he began to talk quietly. "Roz, you're in New Mexico, on the ranch. There was a storm. Everything's okay."

She'd crammed her long frame into the corner of the room, behind a chair, in an obvious attempt to make herself as small as possible. He reached up to tug gently at the covering, pulling it down, revealing her pale, sweat-drenched face, in spite of the coolness of the room.

"You're safe here, Roz," he repeated. "It was just a nasty storm."

Her eyes, those luminous lavender eyes, stared at him blankly, dully, while her wide lips moved in silent muttering. The light threw shadows under cheekbones made prominent by her stress. She breathed out an occasional soft sob, as if she couldn't quite lock away every noise.

Tony's warning from earlier as they parted at the airport came back to Ty with brutal clarity. "Be careful with her. She's not near as tough as she thinks, and she needs someone who thinks of her first. She never will. I can't tell you what happened to her. Hell, I don't know for sure myself. I can tell you she had a shock most people could never deal with."

Ty reached out, thinking to draw her close, but she pulled back farther into her corner. Cold air swirled in through the open door, and he moved away. If they were going to be here a while, at least he could try to make it warmer. "Just let me close the door, okay? We're letting out what little warmth you had in here."

"Don't close it. It gets too dark." Her voice rasped softly, with a quick breath as though she was controlling a sob.

"I'll put on more lights."

"It'll still be dark, and the windows are so small." She sounded rational though the words made little sense.

He looked around, remembering why the windows were made intentionally smaller. Partially to retain heat, but mainly because Devin hadn't felt comfortable in a house with large windows unless they were bullet proof. These windows were Lexan, double paned, bullet re-sistant. But they were smaller. It suddenly made sense why she would choose to sit at his house where she could see out the window.

Frowning, he closed the door, then pulled the drapes. Then he turned on every light he could find and set his hat aside. It wasn't long before the few logs on the fire caught. Eventually, the room would be back to a bearable temperature. He detoured to the kitchen to fill a cup with fresh water.

Coming back, he knelt beside her, taking care not to cast a shadow while he held the cup of water up to her lips. "Come on, sweetie, take a sip. You're fine now."

She clutched at the cup with both hands, took a tiny sip, and held it in her mouth for a long moment before swallowing. Then another one, letting it trickle down her throat. With excruciating care, she emptied the cup one tiny sip at a time, as if water were the most precious drink in the world. Once she was finished, he took the cup away, set it to one side, then reached out his hand to her again. "Want to get up now? Bet you're pretty cramped down there."

She rose on her own, keeping her back firmly against the wall. He kept his face in the light. Gradually, awareness crept across her face, and she pulled the throw more closely around her.

He backed away and she followed, taking small shuffling steps, moving away from the wall to a chair where she lowered herself then tucked her long legs up under the throw.

"Did you eat today after we left?"

She tilted her head as if considering his question, nodded, then frowned and shook her head.

"Just got too busy?"

"Too tired. Took Bailey out for a long ride, played with that pretty red mare you just brought in. Fell asleep sometime this afternoon." She looked toward the curtained windows as though calculating the time passed

"It's not all that late. It's just getting dark earlier, especially with the storm. We don't get much snow lightning, but every now and then it sneaks up on us." As he spoke he moved around the room, opening doors to check the other rooms, turning off lights, and spreading the logs in the fireplace to reduce the burning. "Thing is, it got pretty darned cold in here and it's going to take a while to warm back up." He stopped inside the main room where she sat. "Why don't you come up to the house? There's plenty of Maria's good stew ready to heat up, and it will be nice and warm up there. Don't worry, we have more than enough extra rooms, you won't even know I'm there."

༺༻

Roz wanted to argue. It was impossible for her to ignore him. She would always know where he was. But even that simple explanation was too much for her. Her mind remained in a fog as she watched him move around the cabin, going into the bathroom and emerging with her small toiletries bag, then into the bedroom.

A basket of clean clothes still sat on the bed, and through the half open door she could see him contemplate the pile of sweats, jeans, and underwear before picking up the entire basket, adding the toiletries bag, and heading out into the main part of the house.

"Can you grab your computer and anything else you might need?"

He spoke in a voice so matter of fact she didn't have time to consider what she was getting herself into. Instead, she rose to pack up the computer in a travel bag, then pull on her boots and heavy jacket, before adding a thick scarf and gloves.

⋐⋑⋐⋑

Roz nestled into the deep leather couch, feeling the heat from the fireplace seep into her bones. The heavy wool blanket helped, as well as a good sized serving of stew and biscuits, all eaten in front of a well-stoked fire. It didn't hurt that she could see the moonlit snow through the wide window, and know Ty had intentionally not pulled the insulating drapes. The shivering eventually dialed back to intermittent shudders.

"You doing any better?" he asked into the intimate silence.

She wanted to say she was always fine, but even she couldn't spin a fantasy that extreme. So she nodded and snuggled more closely into the couch. "I think I'll stay right here. It's warm, and I'm about asleep on my feet."

"I'm sure we can find somewhere far more comfortable for you to sleep." His voice deepened and, when she looked over, his expression was intense, nearly feral.

"Are you propositioning me, Mr. Randolph?" she asked with the arch tone perfected when she was a shy young woman trying to make it in a world where she didn't fit.

"Do you want me to?"

She turned away, and considered his question as she stared into the fire. "You know, I'm not really sure. It's been a pretty intense couple weeks. I think if you did, I wouldn't say no."

One side of Ty's mouth kicked up in a self-deprecating smile. "Wow, talk about damning with faint praise."

She grinned and rose on her own, wrapping the blanket around herself. "Maybe I'll hunt up that bed before I make any more of a fool of myself, if you could point the way?" She kept voice her light and shuffled off to the warm bedroom he indicated, only to fall into a surprisingly dreamless sleep, aided by a heated floor and moonlight streaming in through the large window .

❦❦❦

The next morning a note on the coffee maker gave Rosalind suggestions for where to set up her computer. She was soon at work in her usual writing clothes of comfy old sweats and thick socks, with any vague ideas of an intimate breakfast with the handsome rancher relegated to silly fantasies. Ty had made it clear she was nothing more than a guest, and he was the kind of person to be nice to guests. The brief flash of mild flirting the night before was more a matter of her own exhaustion and overactive imagination. Sometimes being a writer wasn't all sunshine and roses.

She ignored the lure of writing about a woman who made a huge mistake, trusted the wrong person, and ended up in a foreign country, alone and scared nearly to death. It was the book her agent wanted desperately, but for now she had another commitment to write as Ross Sommers, the name she used when writing about the struggles encountered by young people on the road to life. Immersing herself in the story about a young man's journey into acceptance and understanding of a way of life totally foreign to how he'd been raised was a balm to her battered emotions. The stories were not always easy to write, but they didn't carve huge chunks from her soul or leave her sitting up at night in the corner of the room, shaking.

She worked most of the day, breaking off to get into jeans and boots and go down to the cabin to sort out what clothes she'd need to take up to the house. All the activity made her decide she deserved a break and could go riding.

She was certainly not expecting to come across Ty, on Mosby, heading in from a day's work—hoping, maybe, but not expecting.

"Well, lookee here, you meet the strangest people out in the woods. Knock it off, bonehead." Ty's mock chastisement was accompanied by a soft slap on the stallion's arched neck.

"I'm just riding along the trail, you don't need to insult me." Laughter tried to sneak out in her voice as she emerged from the woods. Once the gray stallion recognized horse and rider he settled back to a swinging walk, head relaxed, and Ty eased up on the reins.

"You sleep well?" His calm voice made the question seem matter of fact but the intense look he sent her way was anything but.

"Solid through until the morning. Got set up in that northeast room."

"You get much done today?"

"Loads, surprisingly. Enough I gave myself permission to go riding for a while. It's a great day."

"For those who don't need to work, maybe." Instead of the expected scorn, there was a teasing note in his voice, so she chose to ignore his implication there was no work involved in writing.

"I might as well move into that room, and not get two rooms dirty at once."

"As long as you clean up after yourself, I don't care if you use up every room in the house."

It almost sounded like an invitation for more than just the rooms. Almost. She decided she was reading too much into his words as they approached the barn. "I hate to break it to you, but I was not blessed with the housewife gene. Cleaning is something I do when I can't find the floor under piles of mail. And then only when I'm expecting company."

"Your mom didn't tell you a clean house was a healthy house?"

She surprised herself with a peal of laughter. "Only in the stable. At home we usually had to evict a saddle to sit down for dinner. Sometimes maybe a cat." She slid off the bareback pad.

"I noticed you and Tony used bareback pads. You two got a problem with a good Western saddle?"

"We never needed to use them. Too much leather for the kind of riding we did as kids."

"What was that?"

"Pretty much anything that could keep us riding. Jumpers, some dressage. A little bit of cross country." She frowned.

"Something wrong?" He turned Mosby over to one of the hands, who carefully took the reins to keep the stallion from rubbing his head on the young man's arm.

"I haven't heard from Tony. He usually at least texts when he lands." She shrugged, turning to hand off her horse. "You go ahead up. I'll pack up a few more things from the cabin. Just a few," she added when he seemed to be about to offer to help. "The exercise will do me good after sitting on my butt all day."

∽∾∽

When she arrived at the house, arms full of miscellaneous items, she smelled something warming in the kitchen and heard water rushing through the pipes. Ty was obviously in the shower. She was not going to think about steam rising in the bathroom, partially obscuring his wet body. Or about soapy water sliding down his chest muscles and over his thighs. To be very sure, she busied herself at the other end of the house, trying to turn off her imagination.

When he finally came down and they settled at the kitchen table, she made a concerted effort not to notice the damp hair at his open collar. "I don't think I've ever been around a man who can eat more than I do." She mentally rolled her eyes at herself for the odd comment.

"You've obviously never been around a man who actually works for a living."

"I agree you burn more calories on a regular basis. But if you're trying to get me to argue with you about who works harder, someone chasing after cattle and mending fences, or someone taking pictures or creating stories, you're out of luck. Both work eight or more hours, they just use different muscles. So I won't argue, then you can't lose the argument."

"Sounds like you've played this game before."

"Pretty much everything in life is prone to controversy. I've always done what I can to avoid it."

"Sounds kind of passionless."

"Not a bad way to be if you want to live an even-keeled life and not one of high drama."

"Speaking from experience?"

"Considering my friends, and those who over populate both show horses and fashion, no diva can out drama queen a gay photographer or horse trainer."

"So you choose the passionless way?"

"Therein lies serenity and a higher plane of existence." Her attempt to sound serious fell sadly short, and she grinned. "Or at least therein does not lie high drama and emoting in three languages at a party."

He hesitated, coffee cup nearly to his mouth. "Your friends have done that?"

"Some of them lived to emote. Some emoted out of necessity. Some avoid emotions entirely and end up a nervous wreck. Me, I just go along with the flow." She rose to clear the table and, as she reached for his plate, he wrapped long fingers around her wrist, callouses scratching against her skin. She tried to tell herself it didn't affect her. She was going to have to stop lying to herself.

His gaze was uncomfortably intense as he set down the coffee cup. "You've never lost it all for a man?"

She tugged on her wrist. "Couldn't see the reason to lose it all for a man. Could see wanting to share your life with someone, could see building something better than either side of the equation from combining two lives. Could never see forcing the issue. If it was meant to be, then it happened."

He slowly relaxed his hold, but didn't let go. "If it didn't happen easily, it wasn't meant?"

"Not really. If it's worth happening, it's definitely worth working toward and putting a lot of effort into. But if two pieces of a puzzle aren't meant to fit together, getting out a hammer to force the issue isn't the answer."

"What about trimming the edges so the pieces fit?"

"Forcing the fit? Nope, could never see that either. Woman meets a man, he's perfect except maybe he doesn't go to the opera or would rather watch football than go for a walk with her. He's not perfect, he's not Mr. Right, he's Mr. Right Now, Mr. Almost Good Enough, Mr. I Can Fix This if I Try. If he's the right man, he'll want to make her happy and if going to the opera makes her happy, presto bingo, they go to the opera. Not every weekend, sometimes she goes by herself. Sometimes she watches football with him and sometimes she goes for a walk on her own. Because they are, or should be, two complete people who are better for being together, not two disparate beings who can't function without being joined at the hip."

He frowned while his thumb rubbed along her skin and she told herself it had no effect on her.

"So not having found this ideal male who chooses to go to the opera with you, you've remained single?"

"Got it in one. Single, and not ragging on my husband or boyfriend or, heaven help me, 'life partner,' with my girlfriends every time his back is turned. You were married, you must have figured out some of this on your own."

He released her wrist and reached for his coffee. Taking a long sip, he watched her, his gaze never wavering.

When he set the empty mug down, he said, "I'm

coming to think my marriage was as much a mystery to her as it was to me."

"Thus proving out a long-held belief of mine."

"Which is?"

"Readers should never marry non-readers. It's a recipe for disaster nearly every time."

He tapped the edge of his mug and shook his head with a small grin. "You busy tomorrow night?"

"Excuse me?"

"Tomorrow night. It's not Friday, but things should still be hopping down at the pub."

"You have a pub in Willow Springs, New Mexico?"

"You fancy city people call them bars. Somewhere we can go outside the house, get together with some of the locals, have a few beers, some fried food, and have someone else wash the dishes. Oh, and dress casual, none of that fancy stuff you wear around the house."

"Are you asking me out on a date?"

"Not hardly. Just giving you the opportunity for some down home research. Bet you've never been to a real Western small town bar."

"Bet you're wrong, cowboy. Still, I could certainly use an evening away from the ranch. Who's designated?"

"Say what?"

"Who's going to reduce alcohol consumption so they can drive back?"

He frowned then grinned. "We'll play a game of pool once we get there. Winner gets to choose."

The slow smile spreading across her face made him wonder if that had been such a good idea.

"You're on, cowboy."

Chapter 4

Roz looked across the table, eyes bright with mischief, lighting up the dim room. "Rack 'em up cowboy. I'll let you try for two out of three."

"Why do I think I'm being hustled by a pro?"

"Not a pro, just someone who's seen a pool table, and a billiard hall, a time or two before."

Ty leaned against his pool cue, taking in the picture she made in a slinky flowing dark red dress with accents in two other colors he couldn't name. The total package was stunning, something not often seen in this small, off the beaten path bar. "What color did you call that dress again?"

"I didn't. I tend not to name my colors, gives them the idea they have rights and privileges."

He heard a choking sound behind them and turned to see a table of several ranch hands blatantly eavesdropping. "What, you lowlifes don't have anything better to do?"

"Certainly nothing better to look at," the young cowboy offered, grinning while he reached for a pitcher of beer. "You going to introduce us?"

"You think I'm nuts? First night I can get away from the spread I'm supposed to share my company with the likes of you?"

"You know I'd share with you, Ty."

"I know your date would likely be your sister looking for a free ride to the movies, Beau."

Raucous laughter met this sally. Roz blithely ignored all of them as she racked the balls, then turned. "You want first chance before I slaughter you again?"

"You said best two out of three. You didn't say which three.

"However you want to play it." She stood back, giving him access to the table and her back to the observers. Seemingly casual she leaned forward, causing the front of her blousy dress to gap, just enough to make Ty think he might be able to see something interesting.

He concentrated on his shot, telling himself he was too good a player, too focused, to let a little something like some creamy white skin distract him—knowing the entire time he was lying to himself.

He lined up his first shot and watched his ball

bounce across the table and through the scattered balls lining it.

"Too bad, cowboy." She sauntered over with that lazy, long-legged stride and avoided brushing against him. That would be way too blatant, and she'd been the ultimate in subtle. "Let me show you how we played this in Chicago when my mom worked in a bar."

She then proceeded to annihilate him. Again. He avoided watching her rear as she leaned over the table, managing this time to keep herself completely covered but still raising his temperature, and wondered, again, if this had been such a great idea. Particularly since he wasn't going to be able to sample the owner's latest brew.

When she posted the final score, Ty raised his hands in defeat. "Okay, Joe, draft for the lady, cola for me."

"I'll take a small draft, and Mr. Randolph can drink whatever he wants. I'm driving, he's paying." She grinned. "I never have more than one beer."

"Why didn't you say that to start with?"

"I never turn down the chance to hustle someone at pool. Keeps my hand in."

She sauntered over to a table in the corner where the waitress was setting down their drinks, not swaying her hips unduly, but every male eye in the place was riveted on her all the same.

"Something to be said for a confident woman," Ty noted as he held her chair.

She turned her head slightly, looking at him from a corner of her amused eye. "The pool?"

"The pool, the dress, that walk." He strove for a light tone of voice, not sure if he convinced her any more than he convinced himself.

"Something to be said for months of training and years of experience. Some women are born with a sexy walk, some have it forced onto their bodies."

"Which were you?"

"Up to the time I started serious modeling, I looked real good on a horse and was likely to trip over my own big feet on the ground." She settled in her chair. "The basketball and volleyball coaches all got a gleam in their eye when they spotted me in gym class. They lost it quick when they found out I couldn't dribble anything but a drink and got all tangled up in my legs when I turned too fast."

She took the small beer mug, tasted, smiled, and tasted again. "Like a lot of tall horses, it took me a while to catch my balance up to my height. Fortunately, I came across a teacher who used yoga to center her life. She started a study group for those who needed to learn how to concentrate. She had some ADHD kids in there, as well as some who needed to remember which foot to pick up. That class, that teacher gave my life a turnaround— probably my best year of school to that point. Made a huge difference when I was 'discovered' by a friend of Tony's at a show." She looked past the pool table, at the aged beer signs, but he doubted she saw the lighted plastic. "He watched me ride in a side saddle class over fences then walking around later. Said he couldn't take his eyes off me, and he bet I'd have the same effect on a lot of other people. At first, I pretty much ignored him since I didn't see anything attractive about me, except I could ride."

"You weren't suspicious of him, an older man hitting on you?" He sounded slightly incensed on her behalf.

"Nah. It took a little while to sink in, but I realized before the evening was out, he tended to prefer those with the Y chromosome. Besides, he was a good friend of Tony's family, who might have had their faults, but protecting children—which we both technically were at that time—was high on their list."

He lifted his mug in a salute. "And so a star was born."

"Not quite that fast, but yeah my life changed pretty much from that point on. Soon Mom didn't have to worry as much about making rent, could finish up her nursing classes, and get a job outside a bar. Didn't pay as well, but she said she preferred not being the one who served that one beer too many, even if sometimes she had to deal with the after effects."

She grabbed the menu and studied the offerings. "I see we'll be worshiping at the altar of the four main food groups—fat, salt, red meat, and grease. It's a wonder all of you haven't already needed by-passes."

"Hard work and good genes."

"I know for a fact you buy your jeans at the local mercantile, cowboy."

Caught in the act of swallowing the last gulp in his mug, he choked on that one then excused himself to head for the back of the bar. She watched him, noting when he hesitated then slowed to pull his phone out of the waist holder. Phone to ear, he continued to the—no doubt—more quiet area down a hallway.

The waitress came by to pick up the mugs and take their order. Rosalind opted for iced tea, another beer for Ty, and a selection of the artery-clogging but delicious-sounding menu items.

She entertained herself by considering some of the others in the bar as occupants of an alien bar on a small planet in a far distant galaxy. Or maybe even on a space station.

She had nearly come up with an innovative way to produce artificial gravity when the waitress returned with their food. Only then did she realize Ty had not returned.

"You must be that writer who's renting the cottage out at Stormhaven," the waitress said as she set out plates and mugs.

"Must be, at least I claim writer on my income taxes. Not that the government thinks too highly of my in-come."

Tension showed in the waitress's petite features, and she dropped into Ty's vacated chair. She looked around quickly then leaned forward. "You planning to hang around for a while?"

Curious to see where the young woman was going, Roz felt no harm in answering. "My lease is for six months and I'm getting a lot of writing done. Plus it's beautiful country. So, yeah, probably."

"You watch out for Tyler Randolph. That man can charm you without any effort and, when he pours it on, no woman can resist him." She looked over, at where Ty had gone down a hallway, and sighed. "But I gotta tell you, since that wife of his lit out with his horse, he's stayed away from any kind of real relationship. What that woman did to him..." She shook her head and drew a deep breath as if to continue.

Roz raised her hand, palm out. "I appreciate the warning, but I think that's Ty's story to tell. If he wants me to know, I'm sure he'll share." When the waitress seemed to be planning to continue anyway, Roz raised her brows. The waitress took the hint, stood, looked behind Roz, and left.

She could feel Ty's presence before she actually heard him coming up behind her. He eased into his seat and reached for the mug, his face devoid of expression. Then a slight smile lifted one corner of his mouth, and his normally pleasant expression drifted up his face until only his eyes showed any sign of the stress inside him. He turned toward her with a rueful grin and a slight shrug as if to say "sorry." Oh, yeah, he could be a real charmer if she let him. Luckily, she'd become immune to that sort of charm long ago.

"I ordered everything you'd like, which is probably most everything on the menu, you being a hard workin' cow man." She took a sip of her tea, deliberately not mentioning the phone call.

Ty looked at her steadily, and the remote look in his eyes gradually faded. "Has anyone ever told you what an unusual female you are?"

"Oh, yeah. When they aren't telling me I'm not much of a female at all."

At this, he pulled his head back and almost, but not quite, scanned her up and down. "I'd have to disagree with that but when it comes to 'acting like a girl,' you're...different."

"Remember Br'er Rabbit and the briar patch?"

"Sure, kid's book. Talking animals in the South. Wasn't that where the rabbit asked the fox *not* to throw him in the briar patch? So the fox did?"

She nodded. "Since I was, oh, maybe ten? I never let myself fall for the 'don't ask me what happened.' I never did, and it would drive them nuts."

"You think I've been playing head games?"

She hesitated, thinking about the almost lonely look in his eyes and the waitress who wanted to tell all. "Nope. I think you have a right to your privacy. If you want to talk about your call, you will. Otherwise, it's your business."

"You sound like you've lost privacy through the years."

"It's all too easy in those high-profile jobs. Seems like too many people think if you're willing to have your body on display, then nothing is private."

He bit into his burger, chewed, swallowed, then took a sip of beer while he watched her.

She dredged up a bright, artificial smile then bit into an onion ring, finally getting a real smile from him.

"That was Sydney calling. When she first came to the ranch with Mosby in tow, she didn't know her ex-husband was stalking her. Actually, she thought he was dead." He wiped his mouth on a napkin then tried another sip of beer. "At some point, he tracked her sister Lana, also my ex, down where she was living in Utah. He kidnapped her then beat her to find out where Syd might be. Used that to torment Syd during their confrontation."

"I hope you beat the crap out of him." Roz spoke through stiff lips, holding back the horror crawling through her.

"No chance. He fell off the side of a very high cliff before any of us could get close enough."

"Good."

"Lana's been in rehab for a while. Syd goes to see her when she can. I offered to have her come out to the ranch, but she didn't want to leave the city."

"That was generous of you."

He managed a half laugh. "Not hardly. I couldn't see

not offering. I think…" He took a deep breath then let it out slowly. "I don't think either one of us knew what we were getting into. From things I've learned since, Lana may have had her own reasons for marrying me."

"Now that's intriguing. And I'm still not going to ask."

This brought a real smile, and a laugh. "What if I ask you to dance? Can you manage to keep your feet untangled long enough for some two step?"

"You're on, cowboy."

⁂

They managed a dance to one of the Western songs that always pulled at Roz's heart. Something about good choices with bad men, or bad choices with good men. Whichever, it felt good to sway against him, feeling the heat of his large body. All too soon it was time to head back. "Hand over the keys, cowboy."

"I'm good to drive."

"I won the bet, remember? I'm driving or I'm walking."

He studied her face, as if trying to determine her resolve. Taking into account his size, the amount he'd drunk, and the food he'd eaten, he was probably below the legal limit. But a challenge was a challenge, and sometimes she needed to win.

"Spine like a steel magnolia, that's for sure," he muttered in her direction while he dug the keys out of his pocket, keying the lock then opening the driver door before handing over the keys.

The seat wouldn't need much adjusting, and she didn't need any help getting up into his oversized truck, although a boost might have been fun. Their legs were about the same length. She dared a quick look at the denim covering his long legs, as he walked around to the passenger side, and decided his were a lot more pleasant to look at. For her, at least. Once he was in and settled, she slipped in the clutch and eased out of the crowded parking lot, aware of the glances Ty sent her direction.

"So, anything you can't do?" he asked after a while.

"Nothing I've tried lately," she admitted without a trace of smugness.

He let his head fall back. "Confident women sure turn me on."

"That's good to know. I'll mark that down next to your name in my little black book."

He chuckled, and the cab of the truck relaxed into easy silence. All too soon they were pulling into the garage, the door closing behind them. They stepped into the dimly lit kitchen and the warmth of the well-insulated house surrounded them. She let the heavy long coat slip off her shoulders as she eased farther into the room, grabbing it before it hit the floor and folding it over her arm.

"You enjoy yourself this evening?" He lifted the

Western hat from his head and ran his fingers through his thick hair, then settled the hat back on his head.

"Well, it wasn't the opera. Then again, I don't much care for opera so, yeah I enjoyed myself."

"Have to admit I did." His voice seemed contemplative.

"You weren't expecting to?"

"Didn't know for sure what I was expecting. For sure not a pool shark."

"Had to do something to supplement the income and it was darned sure more fun than serving breakfasts to drunks at two in the morning."

They paused in the hallway where they would normally part to go to their separate rooms. She looked up into the shadow of his wide-brimmed hat and met the glitter of his eyes, only to draw in a deep breath. "The night doesn't have to end here, you know."

He stiffened, and his eyes narrowed as she reached up to lift the hat from his head, and place it on the hook behind them. She filtered her fingers through his hair, letting the thick damp strands caress her. Time to show some of that strength he kept admiring.

"What are you saying, Rosalind?"

"I'm saying I liked dancing with you, Ty, and I'd really like a chance to get to know you better." She stood on her toes, but before their mouths could meet he caught her by the arms.

"Better think before you take this next step. I know

you've come a long way from what you were like when you got here, but are you really sure you want to take this step, with me, tonight?"

"I'm the one doing the asking."

"And I'm not one to let a gorgeous woman down. But this might not be the right place or time."

Roz felt the strength she'd gathered melt away. Before she could step back, he stopped her.

"Don't think I'm not interested. But if, when, we ever do get together I want it to be without any alcoholic influence, and when both of us are sure of what we want."

"I am sure. I thought you were also. Sorry to misread the signals." She eased out of his hold, offered him a slight smile without meeting his eyes, and melted away into the dark hallway. Just before she closed the door behind her, she thought she heard a soft thumping behind her. As if he were banging his head against the walls. She snorted a sad laugh to herself, and headed for her lonely bed.

Chapter 5

Ty planned to spend time with Roz, trying to sort out what had turned from a pleasant evening into a debacle. Instead, complications interfered in the day's work, and he came back to the house late. No lights were on, and he didn't see her car in the garage. He hadn't seen her riding out on the trail, and his phone calls had gone to voice mail. The silence in the house reproached him for bad choices, and he flashed back to the look in her eyes, quickly concealed, of disappointment and deep-seated hurt. He stopped first in her room, and some of the tightness in his chest eased when he saw her clothes still hung in the closet though the computer was gone from the work desk, and the whole area was entirely too clean.

He found the note in the kitchen, next to the coffee maker, programmed to start up an hour before, and now full of cold coffee. She'd be back, she wrote in her hurried scrawl. A friend had been hurt, and she had to get to Chicago. She had no idea how long she'd be away. She'd be in touch.

He had a strong suspicion she probably welcomed the friend being hurt excuse to get away. If there actually was a friend. For now, he needed a hot shower to ease the aches of a hard day's work and a solid sleep.

∽∂∾

Ty slapped at the telephone that dared to wake him. Could he reach through the lines to strangle the idiot who thought it was a good idea to blare a telephone ring into his ear? He satisfied his murderous impulses by knocking the phone off the bedside table.

A half-minute later his cell phone chirped from its place in the charging cradle. Recognizing the ringtone, he decided not to see how far he could launch the device. "Yeah?"

"Ty?" Sydney's voice came across the line, with a touch of stress.

He shoved himself farther up on the pillows, trying to rub some sense into his forehead, and checked the time. "You realize it's…past three in the morning?"

"Yeah, what're you doing still in bed?"

"It's three a.m." He pulled the comforter up to cover his shoulders. A T-shirt wasn't keeping him warm enough. "It's dark out, there are no problems to drag me out of bed, and I have a good crew at the barn." Not to mention half-remembered dreams of long smooth legs, gasped mutters, and a compelling face, for once not hiding or overly controlled, invading his sleep. He drew a deep breath and willed himself to pay attention to what Sydney was saying. "You're gonna have to repeat, I missed that last part."

"I said, Roz isn't picking up her cell or the cabin phone."

"She came up to the house a couple days ago." Half-awake, he answered automatically, still trying to get his brain in gear.

"Why? Never mind, can you get her for me?"

"She's not here."

The resulting silence spoke almost louder than her "What?" that followed. "Where is she?"

"Hell, if I know. I didn't know it was my turn to keep track of her." When Sydney didn't come back with a smart ass remark, Ty found himself waking up fast. "What's going on?"

"Put some coffee on, turn on the outside lights in about half an hour."

⟡⟡⟡

Ty was not surprised when he heard the eardrum assaulting thrum of a high powered helicopter. Nor was he surprised to see a dark, predatory super chopper setting down in the large clearing. Two guards jumped out to survey the perimeter before a man of medium height stepped down, wearing what looked like the sort of overcoat worn in the city. That would be Powers. That Sydney jumped down right after him was a given. When Devin didn't emerge from the chopper, Ty moved away from the window and went to open the door.

The guards came in first, nodding to Ty as they edged past. Then Powers, no taller than before, but possibly even more innocuous. Sydney followed close behind. Ty watched the chopper lift away into the dark sky, lights flashing, before turning back to Sydney in silent question.

She shrugged. "Dev wasn't in Albuquerque when I talked to you, so he had to grab another ride." She cocked her head at him. "You know, that one eyebrow thing is pretty effective. You been practicing long?"

"Considering it is now barely four in the morning and the sun won't be up for several more hours, I think a one eyebrow question is warranted. What the hell is going on?"

A low "Clear" came from the guard.

"Well of course it is." Sydney didn't bother keeping her voice quiet.

"Protocol, Ms. Cas—" This time Sydney used the one eyebrow glare on the young guard, who looked away, drawing in a deep breath. "Mrs. Starke."

"How long have you been on Major Powers' security force?" she demanded.

"Sydney, stop harassing the guards." Powers's voice preceded him down the hall. He took a briefcase from the other guard, handing off his overcoat and gloves, then turned toward the dining room.

A gurgle hiss sounded from the kitchen, indicating the fresh coffee was ready. Smiling, Sydney headed in that direction. "Bless you, Ty. Maybe I'll take back some of the nasty things I said about you. Tea, Major?"

"I believe this discussion might call for coffee, thank you." Powers seated himself and began to pull file folders from the briefcase.

"Do I smell cinnamon rolls?" Sydney called from the kitchen.

"Just make yourself at home why don't you?" Ty muttered.

"I will. You still taking your coffee black, Major?"

Catching his nod, Sydney poured another mug, then passed around rolls and coffee, including the guards in her distribution. When Powers seemed to want to open a file instead of talking, they settled in to enjoy the cinnamon rolls. After about half an hour, they could hear the distant beat of chopper blades.

The corners of Sydney's mouth turned up slightly but she didn't leave her seat, even when Devin seemed to be taking longer than normal to cover the distance between the clearing and the front door. By the time Ty heard his footsteps on the porch, the second chopper had lifted off and the first one had come back. Then he heard a second set of footsteps, not as solid as Devin's.

Before he could go to the door, it opened and Devin stepped through, closely followed by another man, not as tall, and with a more wiry build. He copied Devin's boot scraping on the inside rug then dropped his outer clothing on the entry bench. When they came closer, Ty heard a faint "click" and realized one of the man's legs didn't strike the floor with the same impact as his other. The man was underweight and pale, as if he spent more time inside than was healthy. When he sat, he shifted as if finding the least uncomfortable position. Devin stepped to one side long enough to pick up a stool to slide under the table.

"Roberts, glad you were able to join us." Powers looked up to nod his gratitude as Sydney refilled his coffee. She also brought in more cinnamon rolls, which brought smiles to the men's faces. Devin touched her arm briefly and they shared a smile.

When she went back into the kitchen, Ty leaned over to his friend. "Look at you, all googly eyed. You even have little tweety birds flying around your head."

Devin hid his smile behind his coffee cup. "Your day will come."

Powers cleared his throat. "Mr. Randolph, I believe I owe you an explanation about Ms. Summerton's stay here. First, could you tell us where she is now?"

"I have no idea. She left a message that a friend in Chicago was hurt. Might be Tony, she hadn't heard from him."

Devin looked up. "Tony?"

"Anthony Waters, photographer," Major Power interjected. "Childhood friend. They rode in horse shows, stayed in touch through college. She was his first major model and they essentially made each other's careers."

"He came out for a couple of days to do some pictures of a working ranch in the winter plus some scene shots for book covers," Ty added.

"Since when were you interested in photography?" Sydney sounded as if she were on the verge of a good tease.

"Hey, I can pay attention."

"When you want."

Powers cleared his throat. "On the subject of why Ms. Summerton came here—"

"Nothing to explain. She wanted to be someplace cold, so she rented a cabin from me."

"At my suggestion. I felt this would be the safest place for her to stay while she recovered."

"From?"

Unruffled by Ty's sharp question Power said, "Captain Roberts can begin explanations."

Roberts cleared his throat and fiddled with his coffee mug. "My unit got a call for an extraction located in an abandoned, off-the-grid camp in a desert location," Roberts stated with a faint Southern drawl. "After some recon, we located the camp and one live female in an isolated room, apparently suffering from lack of food and water.

"Based on what we found, she managed to suck enough water from the wall shared with the next door cistern. Not much water, but enough to survive, and it was probably loaded with bad microbes. We carried her out to the extraction point after setting up an IV drip."

Remembering her gaunt appearance, the care with which she walked when she first came to the ranch, Ty worked hard to contain his reaction. "Why are you telling me this?"

"You will encounter some people—" Powers stepped in. "—who will try to tell you Ms. Summerton was never kidnapped, never hidden away, never involved in any controversy." He opened the folder and offered a stack of photos and reports.

Ty leaned back, folding his arms across his chest. "No thanks. I don't need to see them. I'll get the story from Rosalind when, or if, she thinks I need to know."

Devin sent him an approving nod. Sydney leaned over to whisper, "Oooh, I'll be sure she knows you said that."

"I'll tell her myself." Ty turned to Roberts and offered his hand. "Sir, I want to thank you for your service, and for what you did to help Rosalind."

A myriad of emotions played across Roberts's gaunt

face as he shook hands with Ty. "Just doing my job. And it's Adam, Mr. Randolph."

"Ty. You know Devin, and Sydney is his wife. You look like you've been traveling way too long. Do you need somewhere to hole up?"

"Funny you should say that." Devin leaned forward. "Seems like too many of the group who found Roz have encountered some problems with their memories. Captain Roberts—Adam—is the one person on the team who could positively identify Roz being in that hell hole. He needs a secure place to stay for a while and to rest up a bit."

Ty glanced down at Adam's leg.

"No." Adam obviously caught the look. "This was from before, on another mission. I strained it a little getting to the extraction point ahead of whoever was trying to stop us."

"Stop you?" Ty asked.

Adam shrugged. "No solid intel on that."

"Windows or not?"

"'scuse me?"

"Do you need to see out or to feel secure?"

Comprehension dawned on his worn face. "Prefer feeling a little more secure. And I'm not a hundred percent on stairs."

"You can stay at the house for tonight until the cabin can be warmed up for you."

Stunned, Adam simply stared. "I can stay here? Just like that?"

"Just like that."

Major Powers rose. "There should be more than enough room. Ms. Summerton is in Florida. I'm sure Mr. Randolph will be leaving as soon as he can pack."

Rosalind was in Florida. Not Chicago. Ty shook his head as he pushed away from the table.

∽∾∾

Ty rolled up another pair of jeans to shove into his travel bag, while Devin watched. "So, you had Roz up here? Was that her idea?"

"She needed bigger windows." At Devin's puzzled look, he explained, "We had one of those thunder snows while I was taking Maria and Tony to the airport. When I came back, I found Roz'd had a meltdown. Makes sense if she'd been locked up in the dark for so long. She was so scared that night—" He shook his head and went back to packing. "She stayed here a couple days before she disappeared. Hell, I thought we had plenty of time. Then Syd called about Lana, and I realized I didn't want Roz caught up in what poor taste I've had in women in the past."

"So you decided she wasn't ready? Learn from me, buddy. You never make those kind of decisions for a woman. You have to have more faith in the right woman. And in yourself."

"He's so right," Sydney said from the doorway, sending a private smile to Devin. Looked like someone was going to get lucky when they finally stopped to rest. "Let's get you moving. Pack what you can't pick up there. I'm getting a bag ready for Roz."

"Where's there?"

"Central Florida. Her phone GPS pinged in Orlando recently. But Ty—unless she got a phone call, there is no sign of any message, either e-mail or text."

"If she said she got a message, she got a message."

Chapter 6

"Hello, Rosalind."

She turned slowly and stared up at him. A trendy new haircut and light application of cosmetics set off her stunning eyes and dark lashes. The shadows under her eyes and cheekbones were there, but not as apparent, particularly in the shade of the clever hat perched on her head. She looked startled for a minute then somehow resigned. "Coming to check on the crazy broad who disappeared in the middle of the night?"

"No, come to see if a friend needs any help."

She sighed. "Sorry, Ty, it's been a rough week. I shouldn't take it out on you."

"Isn't that what friends are for?"

She sat sideways on the wall, pulling her legs up to

her chin, and rested her cheek on her knee. "I used to think so, but lately my friends have been kind of shaky in their support."

"Sure they're friends?"

He sat on the wall next to her, looking out at the pond instead of at the sight of her drawing into herself, the utter loneliness of the pose. Gone was the teasing, confident woman he watched emerge at Stormhaven. He wanted to grab her and hold her close, letting her know she wasn't alone in the world. Letting himself know she was all right.

She didn't look in his direction. "What brings you to Central Florida?"

"Meeting with some people." They decided to keep his cover story vague. "Plus there's a stallion I wanted to see in the flesh."

"Not for the weather?" The afternoon breeze blew warm across the small lake, carrying promises of a later monsoon.

"Not really. I've never much cared for winter that wasn't winter."

"You couldn't have the meeting somewhere else?"

"Nope."

"So maybe Tony got hold of you, said he was worried about me since I took off without warning him either?"

Ty smiled tightly and continued to look out at the lake.

After a moment, she continued. "I thought I had a message from Tony, telling me a mutual friend was in the hospital. Thought it would be a quick and easy trip, zip out, check she had everything she needed, zip back."

"Didn't work out that way?"

"Not hardly. Our friend is not in Chicago, not in the hospital, and insists she hasn't seen Tony and never sent any such message. Nor is the message on my computer any more. But I *know* I saw it." A tremble of panic sounded in her voice.

"I don't doubt you, Roz. You might be absentminded from time to time, but I never saw you imagining anything. Outside your books, anyway."

"You're a majority of one. Everyone else thinks I've finally slipped."

"What about Tony?"

This time she turned her attention completely to him. "I can't find Tony anywhere." She stirred and slipped off the low wall, running her hands down her legs to straighten her jeans. "Since you're probably not here to see a man about a horse, what did bring you here?"

He looked away from perusing her long, long legs. "Do you know a man named Powers?"

"Austin? Otherwise—wait—" She turned slowly, head tilted to the side so the ribbon on her hat hung free. "Little clerk of a guy? Comes across as innocuous until you realize he probably has the fate of the free world in his manicured hands?"

"You summed him up well."

"Writer."

"Well, yeah." Now it was Ty's turn to look out away, searching for the right words. "I met him a while back about…something else. He decided Stormhaven was a good place to know. Remote but with decent access and well-guarded, given who lives there."

"All the vets?"

He nodded but didn't speak.

"So he found that 'perfect place at such a great price' for my agent?"

"And that 'great source of income, won't be a problem' for me."

"Well, he was right about it being perfect for me. Not so sure about me not being a problem for you."

At this he could only grin, turning his head enough to catch a glimpse of her expression. Still tense, still withdrawn. Still not trusting. "You know any decent coffee places around here?"

They found a table under a shade structure, with a backdrop of wisteria perfuming the increasingly warm air. He waited until they were both sitting with drinks in front of them. "Any idea what this is all about?"

"I've been trying to figure that out since I got back from the Middle East."

"Why were you there? Modeling job?"

"I'm pretty much past that, except to help Tony." She fell silent, contemplating a dark cloud in the morning sky, then sighed. "I met a nice family at the Egyptian Event. That's a special show for expensive Arabian horses. Got to know the son pretty well, and his family invited me to visit. Since I needed some background research for a book, I jumped at the chance.

"He was fun to be around, rode well, and could talk on a myriad of obscure topics. He was well educated in the US and in England, but very much a citizen of his own country. Steeped in history, conservative views, Muslim of course but the classic religion, not what we too often see."

Ty felt a stirring, the beginnings of a storm of jealousy. And wondered where this paragon was when Rosalind had been in trouble.

"His family approved of me and of our friendship. He seemed interested and they went out of their way to get us together. It was pretty obvious they were looking for a connection, which is really odd for a conservative family since I'm Christian, though not obsessively so. From what they and he told me, none of the daughters of the better families interested him.

She looked down at her coffee, a wry smile twisting her mouth. "Of course, the fact he was gay could also have something to do with that. My body shape appealed to him and he thought he might be able to go through with the marriage, even conceive a child with someone who lacked obvious female attributes."

She sounded wry, self-deprecating, even humorous,

but there was an undercurrent of self-doubt.

"I think you realize by now not everyone feels that way."

A wider smile brightened her face, then she expelled her breath and went on. "It seemed it might actually work and it was tempting to help him out for a while. I'd yet to meet any man who really interested me. Hamad was charming to be around, and it seemed to be a way to help someone. One thing led to another and we were engaged. They held a big party with lots of happy, relieved family members. I met his lover, Raheem."

She took a sip, then stared into her cup. "An intense young man, very conservative, very devout. Worried about the direction his country and religion were taking toward godlessness and modern living. Thought they'd be better off on the backs of camels, or at most horses, no Internet, no telephones. Mind you, he came from a very successful family so the only experience he had with that sort of life was weekend trips."

Ty nodded. "I know those kind. Think they want to be a rancher but don't know how to wake up without an alarm clock."

She dipped her chin in acknowledgment. "Pretty much. Unfortunately, he had the money and connections to cause some serious problems. He ended up convincing Hamad to go on an old-fashioned raid, and they wanted me to go along. Stupid me, I thought it was a joke, you know, shooting blanks and pretending to raid. Which was how Raheem presented it to us."

Ty frowned, sensing he would not be pleased with what came next. "And it wasn't a joke?"

"Not even. Here we are on camels and horseback, sneaking up on something—a supply depot or another village. Whatever we were shooting, the guys on the other side had real bullets and were not afraid to use them. Half the people in our party went down in the first volley. My horse was shot out from under me, and the last thing I saw was a small missile hitting something that went up in a big fireball.

"I woke up in a small cell in a deserted compound. I could hear some of the other prisoners at first, until a group in uniforms came in at night and used up a lot of bullets. Since I was hidden away from the rest of the party, they couldn't find me. It was probably a week, maybe two before I heard the fabulous sounds of an American Southern drawl telling me he'd come to get me out of there. When I woke up again, I was in a hospital in the US on clean sheets with needles in both arms."

"Hamad?"

"The person who debriefed me in that hospital said Hamad was dead, and he had no information about Raheem. I was woefully ignorant of what was really going on, I wasn't even sure if Raheem really believed it was a joke or he was setting me up the whole time."

Ty shook his head slowly and finished off the cooling coffee "You really don't trust people much, do you?"

She shrugged, and he could almost see that wall going up. "I have to admit I don't have much of a track record for good judgment lately. Agreeing to a fake engagement to help out someone I'd just met seems brainless in hindsight. Hell, I didn't even know I was being set up by your Major Powers when my agent happened to luck into a cabin, not in the desert, where I could write for six months or so."

"'I'd like to think occasionally the angels look out for us.'"

She looked up at him, eyebrows lifted in surprise. "That phrase sounds suspiciously familiar."

He shrugged and tried to look nonchalant. "I found one of your books, or at least 'Ross Summers' in the airport bookstore and didn't have anything else to read on the flight."

"That wasn't one of the more popular books in the series, I'm surprised you found it. Not to mention remembering eleven words out of fifty thousand."

"Well, I'd read the rest of them, too."

Now he had her full attention. "The rest of the words in that book?"

"The rest of the books, or as many as I could find. They're really good, but I'm sure you know that." Finally, he sensed a crack in the wall she'd erected between them—to be honest with himself, the wall he'd helped erect by his actions.

She let out a small breath. "A writer can never hear that too often. Any more than you can hear how great your cattle look, or how good Mosby's working."

He smiled at that but didn't say anything, just kept looking out at the pond. She had to know something else was coming, but he'd learned long before to outwait.

"So, why were you chosen to come feel me out?" As soon as she heard the words, she grimaced. "That didn't sound right."

"At least you didn't say feel you up. What makes you think I was chosen?"

"You wouldn't have left the ranch and tracked me down just to make sure I was eating enough."

"You aren't as smart as you think you are, Ms. Summa Cum Laude."

Now she gave him her full attention. "Tony didn't tell you about that, so who've you been talking with?"

"That doesn't matter right now. Do you know who got you out of that hell hole in the Middle East?"

"Not really. I heard someone say they were there to take me home. I remember being carried, then I woke up in that hospital. I'm fairly sure there were at least four people in the group."

"Carried? Not a stretcher?" He thought of the wiry soldier, and his respect went up by extreme degrees. "Any idea who might have sent the rescue party?"

She looked away. "No."

What was she hiding now? "You weren't even the least bit curious?"

She straightened her spine even more. "All I was interested in was getting away from that place and never seeing sand or pita bread again."

Even *she* didn't sound convinced with her answer, and he knew there was a lot more to the story than she was telling. "When are you going to trust me, Rosalind?"

She looked over, her smile small and wistful. "I've trusted you with more of my memories than anyone else has ever had. I would have trusted you with my body—"

This time he straightened, looking away, then back. There was so much he needed to say, but not now. "That's...something else. When it comes to your memories, you share shallow memories, but not real ones. Do you have any idea why you were in that compound?"

"Didn't Powers tell you? How much do you really know, Ty? I feel like I'm in an interrogation room here."

He drew back, feeling his control slip. "I'm trying to help before anyone else—" He hesitated, looking down before he continued in a quieter voice. "Powers brought someone with him to the ranch, a veteran who told me he was on the extraction team. It seems people are trying to hide the facts behind your abduction or why you were there in the first place. Powers tried to show me pictures and reports of your condition."

"Bet that made for fun reading." Her voice chilled as she lifted her chin.

"Tried." He bit down on his own reaction. He was trying to build trust, not win a war of words. "I wouldn't look at them. It's your private information. When you're ready to share, you will. I was relieved to talk with Adam Roberts and know you had help from a good man."

"That's the Southern-accent man who carried me out?" She frowned. "His walk was a little off and there was a slight noise."

"Prosthetic leg. Doesn't slow him down much. He's staying at Stormhaven"

"You gave him a job?"

"If he wants. Right now he needs to rest, and it looks like he'll be hiding out."

"Sanc—tu—ary," she intoned, drawing the word out.

"If he needs it. Worked for you."

"I wasn't—" She hesitated, drew a breath, looked away. "I didn't think I was hiding out."

"Seems like you weren't, more like Powers was hiding you. When he found out you had left, he came visiting—in the middle of the night."

"Last night?"

"Mmmm, no, night before. I think." He pondered. "Yeah, I slept since then."

"Did you end up going to Chicago?"

"No, Syd had already located you here."

"How did she manage that? Oh, wait." She shook her head and sighed. "Credit cards."

"And the GPS on your telephone."

"Why the spy stuff?"

"According to Powers, someone wants to blame you for everything that happened in the Middle East, while also trying to prove you made it all up. That was part of why he put you at Stormhaven."

"And you're here now because…"

"Powers wanted me to find you."

"Before anyone else can find me?"

He nodded

"Who else is looking for me?"

He was getting an even worse feeling about this situation. "You really don't know?"

"If I knew, would I be asking you?"

"How the hell should I know?" Frustration was sharpening his tone.

"You think I'm a spy?" She drew back then stood so fast her chair scraped back. She faced him with her hands on her hips. "You think I went over to the Middle East to sell secrets or set bombs or somehow do something to harm my country? What kind of a loser do you think I am, for pity's sake?"

"Not a loser but…I don't know…you went over there to be with a local man, one you really didn't care about beyond casual friendship. He had connections to the insurgents or the underground or whatever they call those who don't want us over there. What was I supposed to think?"

"You might have asked me." Now her voice sounded almost sad.

"I just did, didn't I?" He rose to face her, scowling, the coffee and conversation they'd enjoyed now a faint memory.

"No, you danced around questions you never even thought to ask. Did I go to the Middle East to set bombs? No. Did I go there to sell state secrets? The only state secret I know is the state flower of North Dakota. So what exactly do you want to know Tyler Randolph?"

Did her quiet voice hide tears? He hoped not. He didn't think he could deal with her tears. "I want to know why you ended up in a damned prison in the middle of the damned desert." It came out on a near shout.

"Because I was a damned fool," she hissed before whirling around and stalking away.

He stormed after her, capturing her arm in a gentle but implacable grip, stopping her. "Not a real clear answer, Roz."

"All I can give you, Ty." She wrenched away and continued out of the park.

He followed her across the street to the generic big-chain high-rise hotel.

She didn't bother to turn around. "Guess you already know where I'm staying."

"I could say I'm following you, but yeah, Powers knows pretty much all of that."

"You planning to follow me to my room and leave me at the door?"

He winced. "Ouch. I never meant to reject you, babe."

Once they reached the sidewalk, she whirled to face him. "Babe right back at you, sure seemed that way at the time."

"You were there under my protection"

She threw up her arms. "Puh-leeze, this is the twenty-first century. I was there under my own steam and actually thinking about going to bed with a man I thought I cared about. First time in—" She stopped, spun on her heel, and stalked into the lobby.

Refusing to let her escape, he kept pace. When they stopped in front of the elevator, he leaned down and, keeping his voice low, asked, "In how long?"

She ignored him, pounded the elevator button, and jumped into the first available car.

He didn't give up, sticking close. "How long?"

"Too damned long." She looked around at the people who followed them on to the elevator: a middle-aged couple obviously on vacation, in their tacky Wal-Mart wardrobes. She faced the front of the elevator and fumed in silence.

When the doors opened at her floor, she rushed out, Ty on her heels. "It's not a damned race."

"Did you know those people?" she growled.

Caught off-guard, he snapped, "What the hell?"

"Did. You. Know. Those. People?"

"What people? In the elevator?"

"No the ones in the clouds. Of course, in the elevator."

"No, I didn't know them. Don't know them."

"I think I do."

Suddenly subdued, she pulled out her room key then hesitated before she keyed the lock. Forehead resting against the door, she spoke without turning. "Where's your back up?"

He stood to her side and didn't pretend to misunderstand. "Up a couple of floors."

"Am I supposed to come to them once you've weaseled the truth out of me?"

"It's not like that, Roz."

She seemed to deflate, leaning against the door, as all the fight drained out of her. "No? Then what is it like, Ty? What the hell brought you halfway across the country in the middle of winter? You don't even like Florida."

"Well, for Christ's sake, you hate Florida."

"Who told you that?"

"You did."

"Oh, yeah, you're right."

Sighing, she slid her key through the lock then turned so she was looking in his direction while pushing open the door. As a result, the explosion grazed her back instead of hitting her square in the face.

Chapter 7

Ty grabbed her and pulled her down, rolling away from the door. He reached under his jacket before remembering he carried no weapon. He dragged her farther down the hall before jerking her to her feet and into the stairwell. His cell phone rang, vibrating against his chest while footsteps pounded on the floor above them.

"My computer," she whispered, trying to pull away even though she was obviously dazed.

"Not important," he whispered back between clenched teeth.

He led her down the steps at the end of the hallway, supporting her until they were out of sight from the access door. Several people hit the door they'd used so hard it bounced against the hallway wall before slamming back hard.

⁓⁓⁓

Roz looked up into his face. This was not the Ty she'd met on the ranch, no matter how angry he might have been with one of the men or the cattle. This wasn't even the Ty who'd thought she was a dilettante New York yuppie. Nor was this the Ty of a few minutes ago. This Ty was stone faced, tense right down to his bones, and alert to his fingertips. She shivered, leaning against the wall, and only then realized she lost her shoes somewhere. The metal runners on the concrete steps pressed their cold ridges into the bottoms of her feet.

Without looking away from the upper floor, Ty took off his jacket and wrapped it around her. She almost moaned from the warmth, but snuggled in silence. This was definitely not a time for idle chit chat.

⁓⁓⁓

After a moment, Ty urged Roz farther down the steps. A shift in the atmosphere indicated a door opening and closing below them. He stopped outside the next floor access. Holding her back, he eased the door open, peered through, and then pulled her in before gently tugging the door shut. The hallway was empty, the only sounds muted behind a few of the doors. For the first time since they begin arguing on the floor above, he looked at her.

Her dark hair was singed, her face bruised, and somewhere along the way she'd picked up some black on her cheeks. Huddled in his jacket, she was shaking but holding herself together. He slid his arm around her, taking a few precious seconds to hold her close and trying to control his own shaking. His phone started to ring again. Cursing, he pulled it out, looked at the readout, and seriously considered not answering. He knew better, so he thumbed the button. "You have something you want to share?"

"Where are you?"

"Safe, no thanks to you and your elite team."

"Give me a location. They'll pick you up."

"Try again, asshole. We barely missed being thrown through the window ten stories up. What part of protection do you not comprehend? Or was that your little gift that keeps on booming?"

Roz pulled away, confusion on her battered face.

"Is Ms. Summerton with you?"

"Yeah, like I'm going to confirm that when I don't know which side of the toast your butter is on, or who supplies that butter."

"Mr. Randolph—"

"Forget it, Powers. I don't quite have as much faith in you as Sydney does. And considering what you've pulled on her, I'm not sure she's as loyal as she once was."

He shut his phone down before Powers could speak and shoved it into his pocket. "Okay, step one, let's get us out of here."

He headed for a service elevator, tucked away in a corner of the hallway, fortunately found it empty, and hit the button for the lowest floor of the garage. Once the elevator was making its ponderous, creaking way down, he turned to fully study Rosalind.

"The night I brought you up from the cabin, I didn't reject you. I thought I was being noble and not taking advantage of your state of mind. No." He held up his hand when she opened her mouth, knowing she would let loose with angry words, secretly happy she was able to muster up that kind of energy. "I'm not saying you were unbalanced. But you were scared and you were having some kind of nasty flash back at your cabin. Not to mention probably feeling friendless. Tony was gone, Maria was gone, what were you going to do when you needed someone to talk to? And after the pub—I'm not sure I trusted myself right about then."

"You were probably smarter in the long run. I don't seem to be a good risk for long term relationships." She frowned. "Why are you bringing this up now?"

Before he could answer her, the elevator came to a stop and the doors opened onto a dark area. He immediately pulled Rosalind back behind the wall.

"Ty?" A deep quiet voice came out of the darkness.

"Dev? What the hell are you doing here?"

"Saving your sorry ass as usual." Dev pulled them off the elevator but kept his foot in the door opening. "Gimme your phone. You too Roz."

Ty handed his over without question. Roz hesitated then did the same. Devin reached up, pushed the ceiling tile aside, set the phones up there and nudged the tile back in place. Then he punched the button for the top floor and stepped back. The doors of the empty lift closed, leaving them in total darkness.

"That might distract them for a minute. They'll think you went to the roof. Come on." Dev's hushed voice wouldn't carry beyond the immediate area.

With Roz between the two men, they worked their way through the maintenance room, and then into the garage. Ty withheld the questions pounding in his head and concentrated on not bumping into chairs and tables piled on large service carts. Devin grabbed his hand, placed it against the wall, and Ty put his other hand on Roz's shoulder.

She was so slight. Even though she was nearly as tall as he was, her shoulders were only half as wide. But the body under his hand was lean and strong, in spite of the fine trembling he felt and the harsh breaths he heard. And there was no time, dammit, to hold her until the shaking stopped. For both of them.

Dev eased a steel door open, peered through the

crack, then led them into the lowest level of the parking garage. A nondescript beige car waited for them, the trunk partially opened. He wasted no time in yanking the trunk's lid open and reaching in for clothing and a wig. In the dim trunk light, they changed into nondescript style clothes, much the same as the couple in the elevator. Roz slipped canvas shoes on her feet, and he felt some of his worry subside.

Then Dev passed over cell phones and a small packet to Ty. "These have mine and Syd's numbers programmed, and they've never been near Powers and his sneak-ass friends. Since they're not bugged, there's no way they can find you."

"How—"

"Have to tell you later. There's a clean credit card and some cash. Right now, once you're out of here, you're pretty much on your own until we can get away. We're not sure how long that will be. Syd's still with Powers and there's no way to know what he'll be doing next."

"Whose side is he on, anyway?"

"There's so many sides to this damned mess, there's no way to tell for sure. Problem is, they believe Roz knows something she probably doesn't even know she knows."

"Who's they?" Ty asked in an undertone while easing Roz into the passenger seat. She fluffed the curly blonde wig and was busy using hand wipes to clean off the worst of the black residue from her face.

"Our side, their side, both sides, no way to know for sure. But there's a good chance that whatever happened to Roz in the Middle East is following her here."

She looked up at that and started to open her mouth. Dev held a finger to his lips. "No time now, kiddo. Don't worry, we know better." He followed Ty around the car. "Be careful out there, bud. We'll be in touch as soon as we can."

℘℘℘

They left the hotel parking lot at a sedate pace, being sure to exit on the far side of the building from the fire trucks and media vans. As the day edged into night they headed north along major highways, stopping for gas and an occasional break to walk around in an attempt to head off stiffness. Even so, Roz felt like she'd been thrown down a hill then trampled by elephants. In between, Roz pretended to doze instead of discussing Ty's bizarre statements and ended up sleeping most of the afternoon. She woke when they finally stopped at an out-of-the-way motel on a back road in south Georgia.

Ty checked them in to the motel with his hair slicked back under a baseball cap and speaking in a rapid west coast voice. If Rosalind hadn't been so tired, she might have been confused. As it was, once he checked the room and pulled the luggage out of the car, all she wanted to do was fall face down on the bed. First she had to get clean.

Ty brought in the bags, then went for ice, not letting her leave the room once they were in. Whoever shopped for them had been thorough. Night clothes, jeans, and the kinds of blouses she would never wear, mostly polyester blends and fussy collars. All packed into a lavender bag with grotesque cabbage roses. Plus decent quality toiletries. Fortunately she found her own underwear, which meant Sydney must have gone through her drawers at Stormhaven.

Roz yanked the wig off her head and threw it onto the pasteboard dresser while Ty experimented with the television until he found a game. She scrubbed her fingers through her hair, grimacing as she looked at herself in the splotchy mirror. One side was badly singed and there was no sign of the flirty short style she'd sported a few hours earlier. "Might as well shave myself bald. Every time I get started on a decent head of hair, I lose half of it."

Sighing, she grabbed up the toiletries bag and a change of clothing. Soon the bathroom was filled with steam from the shower and she was scrubbing her hair with the lightly scented shampoo. The same scent was shared by the face and body cream. Those choices had to be Sydney's, no guy would have thought of it. She pulled on gown and robe, then came out.

"Why would they have these clothes ready? They couldn't have known my room would blow up. Or did they? Did you know? Is that why you were standing to the side of the door? What's going on? I have to know." She finally stopped for a breath.

Ty swept forward, put his hands on her upper arms, and shook her gently, before pulling her against his chest, arms tight around her back. "Stop and take a deep breath. I'm going to grab a shower and get this stink off me, then we can talk. I picked up some fruit and cheese at the last stop. It looked pretty fresh. Eat something while I get cleaned up." He finally let her go.

Shaking again, she huddled into a chair, pulling the sweat shirt draped across the back over her shoulders for warmth. It smelled like dryer sheets and musty rooms instead of high country air, so she pushed it off. She contemplated the food without opening any packages and finally took a bottle of water to sip. They eaten a bit on the trip, mostly drive through, and she couldn't develop much interest in the pre-packaged food on the table. The television finally caught her attention with pictures of a hotel fire in central Florida. Apparently it was a slow news day across the country. She punched up the sound to learn there were no clues, but fortunately no loss of life.

"Looks like they're not acknowledging your existence if they're not saying anything about the person renting the room," Ty said from the bathroom door.

She turned her head slightly, to see him in a dark T-shirt and sweat bottoms, with his hair damp from the shower. He flicked off the bathroom light and the light of the bedside lamp cast his face into craggy shadows. Rosalind could only stare, as if seeing him for the first time.

Without the wide brimmed hat, shearling jacket, jeans, and well-worn boots, he could have passed for any dominant adult male in excellent condition. His thick hair was pushed back from his forehead and his clean-shaven face could have belonged to someone who modeled with her. But few models, or executives, ever possessed his intensity of vision. Not even the most dedicated exercise fanatics could equal muscles refined by years of relentless physical effort. And nowhere before had she seen the intent purpose he carried in his face.

He stepped forward, into the light, as he watched the television screen that had moved on to both the local and national weather. "We might need to get some more warm clothing, depending on which direction we're heading."

"Where are we headed? Why did we stop here and not any of the other hundred tacky roadside motels?"

"Here I thought you were sleeping over there, you were so quiet. We're in this motel partially because I couldn't drive much farther. Plus, it's a place Dev and I stayed in years ago, a couple times when we were out this way."

"What's out here?"

"Fort Benning Army Base isn't too far. We came out

for training or orientation from time to time. We didn't much like staying too near the base so we scoped out motels close enough to stay in touch, but far enough away not to be a soldier party site."

"You think Devin will come looking for us?"

"I don't know what to expect, actually. All I know is we were having a pretty nice conversation, I was thinking about taking you to lunch, maybe talking you into some sightseeing, maybe a nice dinner and dancing somewhere and then talking myself into your bed."

She avoided a rude snort. Barely. "You don't need to lay it on so thick, Ty. I'm not going to fall apart from your rejection. It's not like it's the first one I ever received."

"I did not reject you."

"Might I point out you didn't exactly drag me into your bed either? It's not like it would have taken much talking, or didn't you realize that?"

"You're pretty blunt." He tilted his head slightly to one side as if studying her. "Wouldn't have thought it of you. Sure didn't show in New Mexico"

She maintained the blasé attitude, with an effort. "There's a lot you don't know about me. Except for that one evening, you didn't exactly lay out the welcome mat in front of your bedroom door."

He sat on the second bed. "So you're saying if I'd been a little more welcoming at the ranch, you'd have been warming my backside all along?" Now his voice seemed cynical.

She flushed and looked away. "There's a huge difference between being outspoken and being crude. You just crossed that line."

"Well, excuse me for not reading that particular part of your relationship manual. Guess we ignorant cowboys just can't deal with polite company."

"Why are you acting like this?" Her voice dropped to a strained whisper as she wrapped the robe belt around her fingers.

He slumped. "I think I'm trying to pick a fight with you so you don't feel so uncomfortable. Same as saying what I said in the elevator."

She was shocked by his admission. "You didn't mean any of it?"

"I meant it. I just picked a time to talk about it when you needed distraction." He shifted on the bed then kept on. "If we have a huge fight, you'll get rid of some of that tension that's knotting up your back and we might be able to salvage some of this time we have together. More likely, we'll get comfortable and Dev will show up."

"Do you think Devin or this Powers person set that bomb?"

"I know for sure it wasn't Dev. He purely hates those kind of bombs, or for that matter any sort of bomb. He thinks they're for cowards and fools. Powers, I don't know. I met him through Sydney. I trust her absolutely, but Powers—"

"Who is he actually? I only have vague impressions from before."

"The head of some super-secret organization that worries about the politics of international balance. I used to think he was one of the good guys."

"And the clothes?"

"The clothes?" He looked confused for a moment, then nodded. "I'm thinking they were worried our clothes were bugged, much like the cell phones. At least yours were. And if we wanted to look like someone other than ourselves we'd need different clothes."

"The condoms?"

He looked away, red streaking along his cheekbones. "You too?"

"A wide assortment."

"Then Sydney must have done your shopping and Dev did mine." For the first time he met her gaze boldly. "I do approve of some of Syd's wardrobe choices."

The robe and gown covered her from neck to toe, in a soft shade of peach she knew helped make her complexion seem delicate and played up her eyes.

She'd learned in the past that being fully covered could entice as much as her barely there warrior queen costumes.

Since Ty had seen both, she wondered if he was using memory to fill in the hidden areas.

"Why don't you stop twisting that belt and come over here, make both of us happy."

"You're pretty darned confident of yourself, cowboy."

"Not nearly as much as you might think. Maybe I'm just real hopeful. And maybe I just need to hold you when we're not worried about the building collapsing around us."

She would have to come to him, make the decision on her own, not letting circumstances take over. No alcohol, no excitement pushing things too far. No coercion on his part.

But the idea of those strong arms around her again, that hard body pressed up against hers, was suddenly too much to bear.

She shifted from one bed to the other.

He carefully leaned back against the pillows with her tucked close to his side. A shudder ran through his hard body as his arms tightened, pulling her even closer. "If you feel this good now, with all these clothes on, I'm not sure if I could survive skin to skin."

Even the thought of believing him brought a warm flush to her body. "Since my skin covers more bone than anything else these days, I'd say your chance of survival would be fairly high."

"There you go again, arguing with me. You sure can be contrary."

"You sure can turn that cowboy talk off and on at

will. Do all the girls down at the watering hole fall for that?"

He rubbed his chin over her short, sad hair. "I've known most of them since junior rodeo, if not grade school. I don't have to work so hard to put them at ease." He shifted and tucked her head down to rest on his shoulder. "Let me hold you, feel your breath against my neck. Maybe I'll get over the thought of you being blown through that window and smashed ten floors below on the pavement."

His arms tightened, and she yielded to his strength, feeling her bones melt against him. The loose shirt and sweats were soft and hid little of his body. Including, she found as she shifted a little closer, a very healthy reaction to the situation.

"Don't pull back now, it was just getting comfortable."

"If I can't go through with the whole procedure, it's not going to be comfortable for you."

He chuckled. "Honey, it's been uncomfortable for me for weeks now. No, keep your head down. If you're not ready, we can still lie here. I should've done this back in New Mexico instead of tucking you in and leaving you alone. Finally figured out you'd been alone too damned long."

He ran a hand down her back, rested it on her hip and pulled her closer. Under the cushy soft fabric her body slowly lost its tension and he rubbed gently at the small of her back. She shifted closer until she all but melted into him.

Roz rested her cheek against his heartbeat and felt safe for the first time in months. In bed with an essentially strange, potentially dangerous man, not sure about her future, possibly in danger of dying at any moment, she felt safer than she had in her high-security apartment. Her eyes drifted shut as she tried to form a sentence.

Ty felt the second she fell asleep. Her body lost all tension and her cheek slid a little lower on his chest. He had an intense discussion with the hardest part of his body, trying desperately to touch the softness so close. Right now the last thing she needed was an intrusion of alien body parts. It was almost enough to have her near, quiet, and safe. Almost.

Chapter 8

Quiet voices woke Rosalind from a dream of being warm for the first time in what seemed like forever. Then the hot rocks she was sleeping on moved and she felt herself falling until she jerked awake.

"It's okay, let me get these covers over you."

A blanket slipped over her body, trapping in some of the heat while the bed shifted. She was about to try and regain her dream when she heard a new, male voice. Her lashes drifted up.

The room was filled with people? As sleep disappeared, she realized the impression resolved into only two, one near Ty's size, one much smaller. They all spoke in whispers but she thought she recognized the voices.

"Syd?" Was that her voice, sounding like a frog in the desert?

Ty moved quickly to bring her a bottle of water, and she drank gratefully. "Sorry, I didn't want to wake you, but we couldn't talk outside and risk drawing any attention."

She sat up against the pillows as Devin took in her robe, and Ty's clothing, and a wry grin spread across his face. "We get here too soon?"

Sydney punched him on the arm and he yelped. Then she moved to sit on the bed across from Rosalind. "How you holding up?"

"Pretty well, considering I don't know why I'm here, who's trying to hurt me, or what's been going on for the past week or so."

"That long?" Syd asked in a reasonable voice, as if they were chatting over lunch.

"I kept seeing the same people in different places, but they were trying to look different. That couple in the elevator?" She looked at Ty and he nodded, suddenly more alert. "I saw them off and on all week. Sometimes a good natured elderly couple, sometimes executives coming from a meeting, one time a sleazy dresser and a hooker. Same people."

"You're sure?"

"My business was bodies and costumes. You can't change ear or eye shape, plus it's pretty hard to disguise your walk unless you're really concentrating. They weren't very good at their job."

Devin turned to Sydney. "One of yours?"

"Not hardly. That reeks of amateur. Or of trying to seem amateur to throw off the scent." She looked back at Rosalind, apparently noting the bruising and dark smudges under her eyes. "You sure you're okay?"

Ty moved onto the bed and slipped his arm behind her, lifting her up against the headboard. "She finally got to sleep when you guys busted in."

"I'm sore and tired, not an invalid." Her creaky voice came out petulant. She pushed herself up farther but wasn't able to move away from the comfort of his shoulder

"You're cranky," Syd said. "Did you eat?"

"Is that the mom coming out in you?" Roz was able to smile a bit this time as a significant glance passed between them. Devin looked over from the coffee pot, caught by their tone. They both looked back at him innocently.

Sydney was perusing the small table, and reached out for an apple. "Here's some fruit and cheese. You want some?"

"Let me get up and move around, I'm feeling kind of creaky." And uncomfortable in bed while the rest were up and dressed. Though she didn't want to move away from the comfort and warmth of Ty's arm, she slipped off the bed, grabbed her bag, and went into the bathroom.

By the time she emerged, dressed in ugly, loose-fitting jeans and an unremarkable sweater, with a knitted cap drawn over her choppy hair, a small meal of sliced fruit, cheese, and bread had been set out. Ty had pulled on similar-fitting jeans and an open plaid shirt over his T-shirt. They ate, the men hungrily, though it wasn't what anyone had in mind for a real meal.

"You know what I'd like?" Rosalind daintily nibbled on an apple slice, then a cheese wedge.

"Shrimp? Caviar?" Sydney asked.

"A Double-Double from In'n'Out. With a milk shake and a couple orders of fries. But we'd have to go to California."

They gaped at her.

"Hey, high metabolism here, guys. And that's the best comfort food I can think of, short of Maria's green chili pork stew."

"Yummm, with fresh biscuits dripping in butter," Sydney added as she scooped up the last of the cheese just ahead of her husband.

Devin sipped at his coffee and grimaced. "Stop the torture, you two. It's going to be a long time before we get any of that."

"What do you know, that we don't?" Ty growled.

Sydney reached for Devin's coffee. "That must be from the last century. Okay." She looked around. "Powers is waiting to meet us."

"He's what?" Ty jumped to his feet, ready to do battle and glared at his partner. "You led him here?"

"No, we told him we'd bring you to where he is. Powers knows he messed up and trusted the wrong people. But he's our best chance to come out of this whole and, in Roz's case, not in jail."

Roz pushed away from the table. "Well, I'm glad you waited until we ate something."

"You're not exactly surprised," Ty noted.

"After what I do remember happening in the Middle East, the only surprise was ending up in a hospital on American soil."

"Which was why you were pulled out the way you were." Sydney lifted her brows as the three sets of accusing eyes met hers. "I'm not holding anything back. I only figured it out myself a little while ago. I think Roz accidentally got herself involved in something she shouldn't have and ended up in the wrong place, wrong time."

Roz nodded reluctantly.

"Then all hell broke loose," Syd kept going. "She was swept up in some sort of retaliation and tossed into a sort of jail, along with a few of the other participants. They figured out who she was, whether it was woman, an American, or the friend of someone, and separated her from the rest of the group, possibly for her own safety."

Roz nodded again and drew her feet onto her chair, wrapping her arms around her legs.

"The first 'rescue attempt,'" Syd continued, grimacing at the phrase, "was initiated by the friends of the peo-

ple who got her involved in the first place, and it was only marginally successful. They got a bunch of their people out but couldn't find her, It's not clear how hard they
looked. They finished by shooting up the place. How
long were you there after that?"

"I'm not sure. Maybe a week?"

By now, Roz had her head firmly planted on her
knees and spoke in a low voice. Ty's arm came around
her, then he lifted her onto his lap and held her. She gave
in to the need to snuggle against him.

"A week without food or water, watching the flies
swarm around the bodies," Sydney asked.

Roz shuddered and nodded, gulping.

"That's enough, Syd," Ty warned.

"The flies were what clued your rescue party in.
They saw the vultures, and then the flies, with satellite fly
overs. It took them a couple of days to get in covertly, but
once they found you, they risked a high-powered helicopter to get you out before anyone knew they were there."
Sydney took a deep breath. "By the time they arrived,
there were no bodies in the compound."

Roz raised her head to look at the smaller woman.
"Wait, where did the bodies go?"

Sydney shrugged. "A couple goats, some other domestic animals. No humans."

Roz frowned. "But I know I saw—" She shook her
head. "Who called them in in the first place?"

"That's the question we hoped you could answer."

Syd's brow furrowed. "The initial warning was the infamous anonymous tip."

"That makes no sense. Hamad's family wouldn't need to call anonymously."

"Have you heard from them since?"

Roz shook her head, looking down and contemplating a button on Ty's shirt. "There's no way they want to hear from me. No doubt they blame me for their son's death."

"Hamad's not dead," Devin told her.

At this Roz looked up. "I saw him shot." She pushed away from the comfort of Ty's lap, stood, and pointed to an area maybe five feet way. "I saw him shot, I saw the blood on his robe. I thought—"

"You thought he was dead?"

"It was all supposed to be a game, a spoof." She turned to Devin, pleading for understanding. "Like those people who dress up in Western cloths and shoot at balloons."

"SASS?" Ty asked, trying to draw her attention.

She only glanced at him. "Yes, them. Shooting blanks. Flash bangs, yelling a bit, and then taking off. Like counting coup."

"Proving their manliness," Sydney said quietly.

"Exactly. Dash in, dash out, have an early breakfast. No one would even know we left the house. I saw him shot," Roz whispered. "I saw him fall and there was blood everywhere."

"You must have really cared for him," Sydney prompted.

Roz shrugged. "He was so much fun. We had a lot in common. He lived every day as if it was a gift. When I saw him fall, I guess I kind of lost it."

"Did you shoot at anyone?"

Roz shook her head, remembering. "How could I? All I had was a sword. You know, one of those big curved blades, like a scimitar." She swooped her hand through the air, mimicking a flourish. "It was so pretty in the torch light, I felt like I was riding to war in a fantasy army."

"Not much of a fantasy if the other side has real bullets," Ty observed.

"I'm not sure they were the only ones with real bullets." She felt the frown pulling at her brow. "Most of the people with us had old muskets—they could shoot but were loaded with blanks, you know, for effect. But I heard—" She hesitated. "I heard something from behind me that was much louder, much sharper. A more modern weapon."

"Any idea who was shooting?"

"No, I didn't look around, just kept riding forward. They gave me a stallion to ride. He was beautiful, but a real bonehead. It was all I could do to keep him aimed straight. The saddle was an antique and not really comfortable." She stared into the dim room, remembering that fateful evening. "Hamad was looking over at me and laughing like a loon. He said something…I don't remember what, probably because I couldn't hear him. Then a red spot appeared on his chest and he fell backward off his camel. I hauled on the reins and jumped off. Got my foot stuck in the stirrup for a minute, darn near got dragged, before the horse went down. Shot. By the time I got free, I was too far away to get back. Someone grabbed me. I fought, but since I was a pretty pathetic fighter it didn't take long for them to tie me up and toss me into the back of a wagon…I think. I woke up in the compound." She shrugged. "Sorry, that's all I really know."

"So, this Hamad. You were really close?" Ty tried to sound nonchalant.

"Nearly as close as I am with Tony, only I've known Tony since we were teenagers. Hamad's family really liked me. If Hamad's not dead, why wouldn't his family tell me?"

"The family really liked you? As in…" Sydney's voice trailed off and she looked over at Ty sympathetically.

"As in they were thrilled to find someone of the female persuasion their son actually liked to be around." Roz shrugged, not wanting to divulge more at the moment.

"He was…"

"Gay? Yep, pretty much. It's easy to think of yourself and your culture as progressive, modern, and open, until your only son and heir can't get turned on by the most skilled courtesans in the country. When he called to say he was bringing me home with him, they pretty much pulled out the fatted calf and started making wedding plans before we touched ground. Then they saw me."

"What's wrong with you?" Ty demanded, defensive on her behalf

"I came off the plane, two inches taller and even more slender than he was, and they understood why he could tolerate me close to him. In their eyes, I had no feminine attributes. How could hips this thin carry a child? But they were willing to accept me if I agreed to play their silly little game and be his pretend wife. Eventually, I was expected to produce an heir but science has a way of making that happen without physical contact. He asked me to play along for a while and keep them off his back."

Now Ty understood all too well how much his restraint had hurt her in New Mexico. In spite of her high-profile life, she'd never been able to think of herself as feminine. He reached out, but was pulled up short by Devin's voice.

"That covers a lot of the questions Powers will ask, but we better get a move on." Devin looked at his watch. "We've got about an hour's drive and it's nearly dawn. Let's get you packed up and out of here."

ﮀﮀﮀ

Silence reigned in the innocuous beige car. Ty drove with his attention strictly on the road, except for glances in the mirrors to check for any other vehicles. Other than Devin's equally innocuous car in front of them, the road was vacant.

Finally she could take no more. "Ty?"

"Don't. Whatever you're going to say, to apologize for, just don't."

She shrank back.

He glanced over then slammed his fist on the dashboard. "Dammit! Why do I always say the wrong thing to you?" He reached over and touched her cheek. "You don't have a damned thing to apologize for, Rosalind." He said her name as though it was a word of great beauty. "Whatever happened to you before we met was before. You had no reason to trust any of us enough to tell us your problems, your troubles. Hell, you've barely met Sydney or Dev. We should be apologizing to you. From where you sit, I bet you think all of this was a set up to get you to confess to getting Hamad killed."

She glanced at him then stared down at her hands, where she'd intertwined her fingers. "There was more."

"There always is, which is probably what Powers wants to talk to you about. So we don't need to go over it right now. We've got maybe twenty minutes before we meet up. I'm going to make sure we don't get separated afterward. Unless you want to go off on your own?"

She shook her head, staring at him with suspiciously bright eyes.

"Don't go looking at me like that, dammit. These jeans aren't made for that kind of temptation."

Against her better judgment she glanced down. Then she let a smile, evil and sweet, bloom across her face.

Ty's large hands clenched on the steering wheel. "Now you notice me. Wonderful. Took you damned long enough."

"Oh, I noticed you before, cowboy. I just couldn't figure out what to do about it."

"Probably what you did with your other lov—" He stopped, as if the most shocking idea ran through his head. He shot an incredulous look in her direction. "No, you can't be."

"Not technically. There was someone back when I was in college, but it only lasted a summer then we both moved on. It wasn't interesting enough to justify the sweat and effort, and I really didn't meet anyone who stirred me enough so I didn't bother."

"I'm betting that's another long story you need to share one day. But not now, when I'm already aching to hold on to you." He shifted again. "Distract me. Tell me something about your childhood."

She took him on a humorous journey through her life as a young rider, willing to do anything to be on a horse and avoid school. Tony was involved in a lot of the stories, including the machinations they went through to keep him from being outed before he was ready. Ty laughed and groaned in the appropriate places and, in general, seemed to relax.

Until he noted, "You spent a lot of time watching out for Tony. That's the same thing you did for Hamad, and it almost cost your life."

She shrugged. "I can't stand back when there's a chance I can help someone."

He shook his head, sending her a look that promised a longer discussion when they had more time.

ოჟთ

Powers had set up headquarters in a hunting cabin at the end of a road worse than any Ty would ever tolerate at Stormhaven. His head tapped against the roof of the car several times, in spite of seat belts and extremely slow speeds. He could barely make out the camouflaged guards and was fairly sure they exposed themselves, either in warning or to let him know the area was safe. With Powers, you could never tell.

Rosalind fell silent when they turned off the paved road, and he wondered if she'd dozed off. As they pulled up behind Devin's car, she stirred. "Looks like he's got a lot of people protecting him."

There was no problem with her powers of observation. "I'd forgotten how difficult it is being around a smart woman."

The passenger door opened as he spoke and Sydney glared at him. "Meaning what, Ty? Before you speak you better remember that I know your deepest, darkest secret, and I'm willing to share it with Roz." Sydney took Roz by the arm, leading her toward the house. "Keep the bags in the trunk but maybe turn the car around."

In case of the need for a speedy withdrawal, Ty realized. He didn't waste time arguing.

⸎⸎⸎

Once inside, Sydney was in no hurry to take Roz farther into the house. She nodded to the man directly inside the door, who stepped back, giving them an illusion of privacy.

"Powers is used to getting his own way, but that doesn't mean he always should. Tell him the truth as you remember it. Don't embellish, don't lie. I swear he sees right through you. He's the one who screwed up, not you, so don't let him try to drop any blame on you." Sydney paused for a quick breath. "Do you want to get away from Ty?"

Roz could only shake her head, covered in the ridiculous blonde wig and bouncing curls. This Sydney was a new person: intent, crisp, with a deadly edge. The door opened behind them, Ty and Devin entered, and she recognized the same aura surrounding them.

Ty's large hand settled in the small of her back, comforting her with its warmth while guiding her as they followed Sydney. "No, you haven't fallen through the rabbit hole," he said. "We can exchange stories later."

⁂

At first, Major Powers seemed harmless. Neither tall nor particularly elegant. Quiet, with an air of competence such as she witnessed in good accountants or mid-level managers. He greeted her pleasantly, half rising while they took seats around the heavy wooden table. Neither Ty nor Devin responded to Powers's suggestions to go away. Instead, they brought chairs from the other room to sit next to the women. Close enough for Rosalind to feel Ty's warmth, greatly needed in spite of the comfortably heated room.

"Ms. Summerton, I have been looking forward to meeting you for some time now."

"I regret I didn't know that. I could have made arrangements to meet with you at any time." She kept her voice calm and sweet, opening her eyes wide in sincerity. She felt Ty hold himself very still, as if to avoid snickering.

"We need to discuss what happened in the Middle East last year."

"I think we first need to discuss why my hotel room was bombed, why I'm apparently being watched by at least one group of people pretending to be what they're not, and why I had to leave Florida under duress. Oh, and while we're at it, can we discuss why my cell phone had a tracker and what you plan to do about my lost computer? I had several major works on that computer."

Powers stared at her, mouth slightly open. Her tone had been sweet but firm, and she had no problem meeting his gaze. They locked stares for several moments before Powers looked at the papers in his hand.

"I believe the matters relate to each other, which is why you need to tell me what happened in the Middle East."

"I went to visit someone I met at an Arabian horse show. I stayed with his family. I met some of his friends. They decided to play dress up, mimic ancient warriors, and raid a friend's compound. Unfortunately, I learned too late that the friend was playing another game. I woke up in a cell in a deserted compound. After I was there for several weeks, I was rescued. What about my computer?"

"You left out a few details."

"My friend's family wanted me to marry their son and were preparing for a wedding when we went on the raid. I thought their son died in the raid, but never heard the details and did not want to contact them and dredge up ugly memories."

"Hamad's family denies any knowledge of you and states he was never intending to marry anyone, much less an American woman who makes her living taking her clothes off."

"You take your clothes off, Roz? No one told me," Devin whined in a loud undertone.

"Underwear model, you idiot," Sydney growled. "And you'd better get those thoughts out of your head or you're sleeping in the car tonight."

Roz bit back a grin at the interplay before she answered. "I'm sure they deny it, but there were plenty of paparazzi around when we went out."

"None who will admit to ever seeing you with Hamad ."

"Sorry, I'm not buying that. If nothing else, the pictures would have shown up on the Internet or in magazines." Roz spoke firmly, hiding the uncertainty that was trying to emerge.

"Again, there is no evidence you were ever in the Middle East."

She blew a raspberry through lips that wanted to tighten. "So some nebulous someone altered a flight manifest, bought or scared off paparazzi, and changed every fanzine website? Why would they bother to do that? Marrying me off to Hamad was his parents idea. I know, you're going to say that, since I wasn't there, I couldn't have been married off to their son. Since I know I was there, whatever you have to say doesn't mean squat to me."

"Then there's the matter of the so-called message you received concerning a friend in the hospital who was not ill or injured and says no message was sent."

"Said message being on the computer conveniently blown up in my room, unless someone took it out when they put the bomb in place. Where's the computer, Mr. Powers?"

"Major," interjected one of the bland faced men standing around the room.

"There was no indication of said message on your server." Powers continued as if there had been no interruption.

"Fine, so I'm up against hackers far beyond the ordinary. Give me my computer and you won't have to worry about me anymore."

"I'm afraid it goes a bit further than that. Due to the assertions of Hamad's family, our State Department is actively looking for you. As well as the Defense Department and no doubt Homeland Security as well."

"CIA, FBI, and all the other TLAs? That's Three Letter Agencies, in case you're wondering. What the hell did I do to get every incompetent branch of our government after me?"

"According to them, you planned and staged a raid on a compound and, during said raid, you killed a son of one of the top officials."

"How could I do that when I wasn't there? Did I kill him with that ridiculous sword?"

"He was killed by a machine gun."

"Bit late to look for GSR, I guess." She felt her eyebrows pull together. "And I thought he wasn't dead?"

"Hamad's not dead. We can't say the same for other members of your team. And you are being remarkably calm about these accusations, Ms. Summerton."

"Not. My. Team. I saw people cut down on both sides of me during that so-called fake raid. People I'd been joking with ten minutes before, who were no more prepared for an actual fight than kittens up against a pack of wolves. They were torn to shreds. No doubt someone's son did die. I was sure Hamad had died until this evening. Whose son?"

"Raheem something or other."

"Really? Did anyone actually see his body?"

"Why do you ask?"

"Because the raid was Raheem's crack-brained idea. According to him, he set it up with the son of the head of the compound we were 'mock' raiding. He got the weapons, and some of the horses. In fact, he made sure I rode the bone-headed stallion that tried to throw me the whole time we were racing across the desert."

Powers held up a grainy photo. "This man?"

Rosalind looked closely at the photo then took it out of his hand. "Where did you get this picture? And don't tell me you have your sources, I know that. Which one told you they took this picture?"

"An interesting way to phrase the question. Someone sent a media card to one of our contacts. Why?"

"I took this picture. See the shadow here? That's a tree in the back yard of Baheera's house. We went there for dinner, and I was goofing around with my camera, taking pictures of the people. Most of them were posing and having fun. Raheem was laughing a few minutes before this. I didn't realize who was in the background until after I shot the picture." She stared at the picture while frowning. "My camera was with me when I woke in a US hospital, along with everything I took with me to the Middle East, but no media card. And nothing I acquired there. I guess if I was never there I could never have acquired anything or taken any pictures."

"Who's with Raheem?" Powers asked after she stopped talking.

"That's Mansur. I think he went to school with Raheem and Hamad."

"Did you speak with him?"

"Not much. He wasn't real fond of American women."

"Or of Americans in general. He's the head of a terrorist group. He went missing shortly after your night raid and hasn't been seen since, anywhere. There's a good chance his group is planning something in the US and you're the only person who might know what."

She settled back, staring at the picture. "So that's why he was such a butthead. I thought he just didn't like women at all, instead of didn't want to be around me in particular." She handed the photo back. "Nope, don't know a thing about it. Will you give me my computer so I can go now?"

"What makes you think we have your computer?"

"Given how many people have been watching me the last week, most of them paid by my excessive taxes, I kind of doubt anyone other than your minions could have gotten into my room. No doubt the room was wired for sight and sound, so even if they had snuck past whatever guard you had on the door, they would have been seen inside the room. By the same token, only your group could have gotten into the room to set any kind of explosive. Ergo—and I've always wanted an excuse to use that silly word—you took what you wanted before you destroyed the rest."

"There's nothing on your computer beyond your stories."

She threw up her hands. "So you do have it, and you have no reason to keep it."

"It's evidence in a potential terrorist plot."

"If there's nothing in there but my stories, then how could it contain any evidence?" She leaned forward, barely controlling her reactions. "Look, I know Homeland Security has been casual about that silly piece of paper called the Constitution, but you still need to establish a crime before you can manufacture evidence."

"And you thought she needed protection from me?" Powers looked around and sighed. "Ms. Summerton, we need your cooperation, or we could be facing a monumental tragedy."

"Mr—Major Powers, did you ever think to ask instead of manipulating?" She let her anger out now, narrowing her eyes, looking around the room at the guards then starting to rise from her chair. "I've had it with people, whose job descriptions include protecting our citizens, going off half-cocked, threatening, and manipulating to their heart's content. I don't know who has been messing with my computer and, since you won't turn it over, I won't ever know. At one time, I thought that kind of bullshit didn't happen in my country, but I'm obviously very wrong. Just because you've learned to be paranoid doesn't mean Big Brother isn't watching every time you buy one bottle of wine too many or check out the new gun store in town."

Powers waited to be sure she'd finished before continuing.

"We need to talk to someone who has been in the Middle East recently and in the homes of these people."

"What about Baheera? She went pretty much everywhere, and I'm darned sure she wasn't nearly as flaky as she pretended."

"She is a possibility but, at the moment, she's not available. It seems she contracted a virus and hasn't been well."

Roz sat back, feeling ill. "How many of those people I hung out with have disappeared?"

"Most, if not all, of them."

Powers voice continued to seem remote but she thought she heard an undertone of sympathy. No doubt her imagination was working overtime. "And Hamad is alive and with his parents?"

"So far as we can tell, yes. Preparing for marriage to one of his cousins, which the family says has been planned for many years. They were waiting for the cousin to grow up."

"She's going to grow right out of the family, if it's the cousin I'm thinking of. He refused to marry her before, said it wouldn't be right. First off, because of their close relationship but also because she wanted to see more of the world, maybe go to college in the US." She hesitated. "What about my passport entry into their country?"

"Since you were never in the country, they claim your passport must have been stolen."

"I hope nothing happened to the people who pulled me out of that hell hole."

"Not much can happen to them. They're highly trained and, as far as the world knows, they don't exist."

"Cool, the Men in Black do exist. What about this Roberts who helped me? Why are you hiding him out at Stormhaven? Is Stormhaven your Fortress of Solitude?"

That earned her a slight twitch of his thin mouth and the echo of a throat clearing.

Chapter 9

Y ou keep that up, next thing you know, you'll be working for Powers." Sydney peeled the cover off her straw, stuck it in the milkshake, took a deep pull, then sighed in contentment.

"How do you put up with him?"

"Powers? He's a manipulative irritating pain in the rear. But he's also works pretty much twenty-four/seven, trying to keep the world from blowing itself up. I know, he messed up with you, but he was working from incomplete or false information, though it did seem odd you weren't killed in that raid. The outpost where they found you belonged to the bad guys, and I've no doubt the call came from someone in that group. You've been set up, masterfully. Eat up, you'll need your strength."

Roz hesitated then reached for one of the many bags

brought in by Devin and Ty while she was in the shower. She looked around the shabby room, while unwrapping a cheeseburger, and finally took a small bite.

"Powers figured that out more quickly than you realized," Sydney continued, "but he played along with the other group long enough to find out what they knew, until he could meet you in person and decide if he needed to take you out of the game or use you."

"As he's used you and Devin?"

Sydney shrugged. "I've let him use me. There are some things about my past I'm not real proud of. To my mind, working with Powers is my way of paying off a lot of bad karma."

A quiet knock at the door preceded the lock releasing to a room key. Ty and Devin slipped in, carrying the rest of the luggage.

"We're staying here tonight?" Roz tried not to sound as dismayed as she felt. "If we are, we'll need to bring in more food. There's a colony of roaches in the bathroom that will need sustenance."

Sydney put down her milkshake, half rising to turn in her chair. "Oh, ick."

"Calm down," Devin said. "We needed to get the rest of the stuff out of the cars. Powers is having something a bit more upscale brought around."

"You're trusting something he's providing?" Roz asked, letting her eyebrows raise in question.

"As long as it's directly from his team, the only tracers will go back to him."

"That's damning with faint praise." Roz took another small bite of the cheeseburger.

Ty chuckled and reached for his bag. "Is the food okay?"

"Not In'N'Out, but also not a major chain."

"Aren't you hungry?"

"I think I'm too tired to be hungry," Roz admitted, setting down the food. She managed a small smile. "But I'm betting there's not enough time to get a nap, and you all need to dig more information out of me."

"They said no more than twenty minutes for the new vehicle," Ty said around a mouthful of food, chewing with determination if not pleasure.

"In the meantime, we're going to use you up," Devin promised. "You can sleep later. The new hotel's no more than an hour away, well-guarded, and out of sight, according to Powers. We'll stay there for a couple of days."

Sydney wasted no time with the promised grill session. "Something else we need to consider is where Tony stands in all of this mess."

"More to the point, where he is period," Roz muttered.

"You haven't heard from him?"

She shook her head. "Not since he left the ranch. Ty took him and Maria to the airport. I didn't even hear from him when he landed in New York."

"Is that usual?" Sydney asked, squirting out a small puddle of ketchup.

"With Tony, it's hard to say what's usual. It depends on where he stands with his latest lover, or what kind of project he's involved with. He can get fairly intense and lose track of time or other people. I usually hear from him when he wants something."

"We have no record of Mr. Waters after he boarded the plane in Denver."

Stunned, Rosalind croaked, "Airport cameras?"

Sydney grimaced in sympathy at Roz's reaction. "Not conclusive. Several people deplaned who resembled him, and they walked in a group." Sydney hesitated, then took a deep breath. "Who introduced you to Hamad?"

"We met at that Arabian horse show. I went there with Tony but…" Her voice petered out as the full implication of what she said came home. "No. I cannot—I will not—believe what you're saying. Tony would never do anything to hurt me."

"What about hurting his country, or those who've hurt him, or stood in his way, or threatened his friends?"

She looked away, thoughts jumbling. "Who do you mean?"

"We found records dated a few years back, where Mr. Waters had an unpleasant encounter with an agency," Devin said, drawing her attention. "He was personally and professionally threatened and, in return, he made some inflammatory statements." He frowned then slapped at his vest pocket. Pulling out his phone, he stood, moving away from the table.

Roz looked back at Sydney, working hard not to let her anger spill over. "He was royally pissed, and rightly so. They interfered with an important contract, not to mention they endangered a group Tony worked with for years. It's not like he has any reason to trust most government agencies."

"Would that be enough for him to attempt to get even with the group?" Sydney pressed.

Understanding how important her answer was, Roz thought it over. "I can see him wanting to get even, but I can't see him hurting me in the process. Any more than I could hurt, or betray, him." She looked around, letting them see her resolve.

Ty placed a supporting hand on her back and, after a minute, she relaxed, allowing herself a small smile.

Sydney took a moment then asked, "If you don't consider Mr. Waters to be part of whatever is happening, do you think it's possible he's in danger?"

Roz tilted her head, feeling her way through her answer. "Tony can be pretty wild sometimes, in your face if he thinks his sexuality offends. He wouldn't have involved me or called me if he thought it could have been dangerous. He was really upset about what happened with Hamad. But—" She stopped, frowning as she ran through the possibilities. Finally, she shook her head. "No, no matter how pissed off he might be, I can't see him doing something to harm his country"

Ty stroked his fingers along her shoulder. "Could he have been misled or tricked?"

She shrugged. "Anything is possible. He can be hot headed, but only in certain situations, generally when a friend is threatened."

Sydney leaned in farther, eyes boring into Roz. "If you were threatened, would he react differently?"

She shook her head vehemently. "Risk the country? No. Not even then."

"Then where is he?" Sydney demanded.

Roz ran her fingers through her hair in frustration. "I don't know."

"What about the message stating your friend was in an accident and in the hospital?" Ty interjected. "Any chance that could have come from Tony?"

"No. Tony's never been fond of practical jokes or playing games. It's not his style."

"Even to keep you out of harm's way?" Devin asked as he came back to the table. "That was Roberts on the phone. They stopped a group on the way to Stormhaven." Seeing Ty's frown, he rushed on. "Don't worry, no one got close to the ranch. They were sort of wandering around lost when the sheriff decided to check out the rental full of strangers." He turned his attention to Roz. "If Tony somehow knew they were coming after you, what would he do to help get you out of there?"

That was easy to answer. "Call me, tell me there was trouble and to get out."

"What if he couldn't tell you that directly? Would he use subterfuge to move you?"

She nodded slowly. "He'd do whatever it took to get me to move, and yes, telling me Sandy was in the hospital would make that happen." She folded her arms and glared. "Then again, why wouldn't he just tell me it was dangerous and I needed to leave?"

"Maybe he couldn't?" Devin suggested.

Ty tilted his head as something caught his ear. A minute later they all heard the growl of a large engine. "Grab the food, it looks like we're blowing this fire trap." Then he grimaced, no doubt remembering what happened the last hotel they evacuated.

Sydney laid her hand on Roz's arm. "I hope Tony is as loyal to you as you are to him." Her voice was low and carried a thread of sympathy.

∽∾∽

Ty watched Roz smooth cream into her skin, absorbing the way the cream went from white to nonexistent and how she gave her entire attention into ensuring each patch of skin was covered.

As if feeling his gaze, she looked over her shoulder. "What?"

He should have said "nothing," but his voice

wouldn't obey. What came out instead was, "Were you always so girly?"

She straightened, her eyes frowning. "Since I was born a girl, pretty much yes. If you mean did I always fuss with myself, that was one of the hardest things for me to learn. So many other models learned their beauty routines practically from the cradle. I had to force myself to make skin care a part of my life." She grimaced. "Along with constant visits to the beauty parlor and all those other things we do to keep the economy going."

"Didn't your mother teach you?"

Her eyes brightened as her mouth spread in a wide grin. "Mom was the original 'lay it on with a trowel' beauty expert. She never met a mascara wand she didn't worship, bless her country heart. I'm surprised the hospitals didn't ask her to tone it down a bit, but apparently, since she wasn't surgical, it wasn't much of a problem. The patients didn't mind a nurse with artificial lashes. Eventually, she took a job as a nurse at a correctional institute. They were so happy to find someone who could work with the inmates, they didn't care how she kept herself."

He looked up, momentarily distracted from watching the cream melt into her long legs. "Wasn't that dangerous?"

"When she took the job, I thought so, but it was the best pay she could get. She told me her patients were all grateful to her for being there and caring for them, so if one did get too rough, the others would take care of him for her." She stretched her leg, tilting her head as if checking out the lean muscle under the smooth surface.

Arching her foot drew his attention back to her legs, his imagination back to how those legs would feel—

"You did it again," he almost growled.

She closed the lid on the jar and set it aside. "Did what? Put lotion on the same spot? These past few days I haven't been keeping up as well as I should with skin care."

"Distracted me with your…" Unable to find the words he needed, he waved his hand in her direction. "It's like women learn that in the womb." As he heard the words fall out of his mouth, he groaned.

Roz straightened, soft curves making way to a straight back and high held head. "Excuse me? Since when did you become the great authority on women? Except maybe to drag them into bed, or is that only all part of the urban legend? I have to say this is a pretty poor seduction method."

"I'm not interested in seducing you, Rosalind."

She offered him one tight nod, face turned away. "That's been obvious for a while now."

"You're misunderstanding me, again. I'm not interested in seducing you, but I've wanted to make love to you damned near since the first time you stood up, and I looked into your eyes. I've wanted the right to touch your skin and find out if it's even softer under your shirt."

She tilted her head, looking at him from the corner of her eye, now luminous with what he was afraid were unshed tears. He slid his hand around to the back of her neck and pulled her slowly, inexorably, toward his mouth. "I'd ask you what you wanted, what made you feel good, but I have a feeling you wouldn't tell me."

"I'm not sure I know." Her voice was low, husky, uncertain.

"I kind of figured that out."

She edged in his direction until their breath mingled. "I've wondered for a long time if maybe I worked so well with gay guys, because I'm not far from that myself."

"When did you decide you didn't lean that way?"

"When I watched a cowboy walk up a hill and wondered what his butt would feel like under my hands." She closed the distance between them. Their mouths touched lightly, and she pulled back to look into his eyes, letting him know this was what she wanted. "When I watched him ride his stallion and suddenly understood what all my romance writing buddies were talking about. Wondering if your hips would move the same way in bed as they did on the horse. Watching the way your muscles flexed when you lifted a calf up out of trouble. Wondering if you would ever touch me the way you touched that scared filly." She nestled her neck against his hand, looking directly into his face. "Ty, I realize, whatever your reasons, you don't want to seduce me. So I am trying as best I can to seduce you."

☙❦❧

Roz held her breath, hoping she had not horribly misread the situation. Then she felt his other hand slide around her, down her back, pulling her closer, offering comfort and encouragement. His fingers slipped under the sweatshirt and traced back up, warm against her skin. He absorbed her shudder and answered with one of his own. His large calloused hand rested against her spine, nearly spanning her ribs.

"Oh, yeah, you're every bit as soft here as on your face." His fingers slipped up to cup the back of her head, spearing into her hair and he tilted his head slightly. This time when their lips met, they opened and her arms slipped around his neck, giving his hands full access to her body. When he lifted his head, his eyes glittered and his voice was rough. "Do we both want to satisfy our curiosity? Is that what this is all about?"

She pulled back, disappointment stiffening her back. "You think you're my science experiment?"

He winced. "I think I need to keep my damned mouth shut. Or at least keep the wrong words from falling out at the wrong time. Come here." He pulled her close again and they stood hip to hip while his mouth settled back against hers.

For a moment, it was unbearably sweet, learning each other's taste and textures while the world outside disappeared. Then Rosalind edged a little closer, opened her mouth a little more, and reached out with her tongue to taste him more fully. In a flash, she found herself engulfed in his arms, tucked tight against him until she felt nearly absorbed by him. Of their own volition her hips sought the strength of his and she reveled in the rigid shape she felt against her stomach. Rising on her toes, she sought to mesh more completely.

Ty lifted his head, his breathing heavy. "Whoa, that damned near got out of hand."

She leaned back, trusting the steel-hard arm around her waist. "That would be so bad?"

"Depends on where you're at right now."

"In this room. In your arms." She tilted her head, looked him straight in the eyes. Passion clouded them, yes, but clear purpose shone out. The moment stretched out, then his lips lifted in a smile of pure devilment and she understood what the women had been talking about when they warned how he could charm them with a look.

"In that case…" His hands swept up her body, lifting the sweatshirt over her head and off her arms before her next breath. "…I'd say you're wearing a few too many clothes."

He looked down, taking in her peach-colored bra, and she was suddenly very glad Sydney dug deep when packing, since her day-to-day bras were more workman-like than pretty. Frantic to feel his skin against hers, she pulled at his shirt, helping him strip it off. The first touch of skin to skin, his heated to near-furnace-like levels, made her moan. She laced her arms under his and took hold of his hard muscled shoulders while she leaned into his chest. The feel of the hairs on his chest against her smooth skin brought another moan.

"Let's not rush things yet. Let me…" He unhooked the bra and loosened her arms to let the straps slip down then pulled her back. "Oh, yeah, just like I thought." His arms enfolded her again, this time with nothing between their bare skin, and a shudder shook his powerful body. "Honey, I hope I have the restraint to hold off long enough, but right now I feel like I'm gonna pop or go blind." He rubbed his hands down her back, lifted her hips and pulled her more firmly against his erection. "Oh, yeah, that's the way."

Rosalind felt a rush of heat and strove to get closer…closer…there. And, for a moment, she held herself very still against him while small tremors tracked through her body. She slipped her hands under his waistband, too impatient to find out if that bulge was for real or if she was just dreaming. Her fingers plucked at his zipper.

"Whoa up there, sweetheart." He reached down to pull back the bed covers and nearly tore the sheets off the bed. "You want to be a little careful down in that area right now."

Straightening, he unbuttoned his jeans and eased the zipper down. She pushed at his jeans, sliding them down his legs while she sought out his butt. "Oh, yeah, absolutely."

"What's that?" His breath, then his lips, brushed over her mouth.

"It does feel every bit as good as it looks."

Laughing, he lowered her to the bed, sliding off her sweats and his jeans in record time, taking a second to pull out condoms before dropping the jeans on the floor in a tangle of denim. Then he leaped into the bed like an eager puppy, snuggling them under the covers.

Now their bodies pressed together along their entire length and she felt the wondrous similarities and differences. He snuggled his arm under her back, pulling her closer to his side while his hand stroked possessively toward her breast. The first feel of his calloused fingers on her tender skin nearly made her jump out of bed.

"I gotta see this." He pushed back the covers to watch his sun-and-work darkened fingers against her paler skin. Using his fingers, then his palms, he stroked and caressed until her entire universe concentrated on the one spot he didn't touch, until his warm moist mouth settle around her nipple, his cheek stubble brushing her delicate skin.

Rosalind arched off the bed, clutching at his head while her entire body reacted. Writhing to get closer, her legs tangling with his, desperate to connect, to go over or between his, to do something, anything to reduce the frustration.

"Dammit," he whispered, this time in the softest tone she'd ever heard from him, while fumbling with the condom. "Sorry," he muttered, before reaching down and drawing her leg up over his waist. With a flex of his hips, he slid into her body.

His body was an invasion then, after a minute, became the most intimate connection she'd ever felt, minimizing the pain she'd forgotten she might feel. She expected him to rise up over her, to dominate, but instead they connected on this deeper and more satisfying level. Never once did he overpower her. She flexed, trying to draw him in deeper, secretly delighted when he groaned.

"Careful, I'm not holding on by much right now."

"Why should you?"

"I want this to be as good for you as I can make it"

"Make it much better and I might…" She wiggled closer, trying to find the spot that ached the most, trying to scratch an itch deep inside she'd never felt before. Then she found it. "Oh, yeah," she breathed.

"That did it." His hips plunged and he gathered her even closer until their bodies ground together briefly before separating, then returning to full contact. It took only a few hard strokes before she tensed and convulsed, a flush taking over her body, and he followed her into ecstasy. He cradled her against his sweating body, pulling the sheet up and over as he held her closer. "So much for my powers of seduction."

"Don't know what you mean. I certainly feel more seduced than I ever have before."

"I should have taken a lot longer with you. It should have been better."

"Better would have probably given me a coronary."

He drew back enough to look into her drowsy eyes, to read the truth of what she said. Then shook his head. "Amazing."

"What, that someone who takes her clothes off for a living is so easily satisfied? That someone whose eyes are purple doesn't have the IQ of an eggplant? That someone who hasn't had sex in decades, still remembers which parts go where?"

"Someone who is damned near a virgin is so incredibly sexy."

"Oh."

"Decades?" His eyebrow raised as if questioning her accuracy.

"Something like that. Long enough, I can't remember the last time."

He laughed then, a rumbling roar that shook the bed and her, then rolled over on top of her. "Next time, we do it this way." He watched her face closely, until she reached up to loop her arms around his shoulders. "It's going to be like this. I'll use my elbows to keep my weight off you, but I'll let down enough to feel every luscious inch of you." He slid slowly along her body, feeling her yield then tense in growing passion while her soft skin caressed him from shoulders to knees. He leaned down for a kiss, then rolled until she was once again tucked against his side. "We'll try it with you on top once we're in a warmer room. For right now, you'd better stay still if you want to get any sleep at all tonight."

She agreed with a sleepy grunt and felt the room go dark around her.

⟡⟡⟡

Ty left the bed long enough to use the bathroom and paused to stare at the unkempt man in the vanity mirror. Gone was the easy-going rancher known for his humorous ways. And he didn't see much of the angry abandoned husband who missed his horse more than his gorgeous, but admittedly not well-understood, wife.

In their place, he saw the man he'd once been, refined down to reaction and cunning, with a new look. One of determination to protect what was his. He turned off the light and slid back into bed before his body cooled down so much he would chill Rosalind. From now on, his life's work would be standing between her and the rest of the world, protecting her from all harm.

Chapter 10

W e haven't had much time to catch up. When did you leave the ranch?" Ty asked Devin as he sat down at the table in the hotel dining room and reached for the coffee pot.

"Shortly after you did." Devin nodded and moved his cup over for Ty to pour. "Maria's back. She brought her sister and the kids. Jamie's in charge. It's getting to be like he practically runs the place anyway. Looks like Roberts is going to fit right in, even if he doesn't know one end of a horse from the other." He sipped at the coffee, taking a moment to appreciate the quality. "Now that's more like it. The coffee in the rooms is not worth heating the water."

"Sydney complaining?" Ty asked, while closing his

eyes to appreciate the aroma and taste of the rich brew.

"Lately, she's been drinking this herbal tea. She claims it helps her concentrate."

Ty felt his attention shift abruptly to his partner. He felt his mouth stretch into a smile. "Does she now?"

"What are you grinning about?"

"Nothing much. Just looking at a happy man."

"Of course I am. I married her, didn't I?" Devin shook his head, sent a quick glare across the table, then continued. "You had a call from someone in Montana. He wants to send some mares to Mosby if you won't give in on collecting and shipping."

"He knows the answer to that. You get better foals with a natural cover."

"Says the Luddite. Anyway, the old fool deserves some fun since you're the one collecting the dough."

Ty grinned. "Maria's okay?"

"Yeah, she convinced her sister to call the cops in early and didn't let things escalate. It didn't hurt that Jamie was parked on the street or nearby the whole time. He drove them all straight back. Damn he was ripe. There's no telling how they managed to stay in the car with him."

Ty paused, tilting his head while imagining the scene. "Guess he'll need a raise."

"Bet he won't take it," Dev said. "Bet we can get him a job with Powers for a while. He's no more ready to settle than you are."

"I like the ranch," Ty protested then wondered if he meant that as much as he once had. How long would Roz want to stay there? And if what he suspected was true—

"You needed it for a while, same as me. It doesn't hurt that we have it to go back to, but it's not for us to stay there full time. Not yet anyway." Devin looked over at the entrance, and his face softened marginally. "It's probably not just our decision anymore."

They watched the women come into the dining room, Rosalind's head tilted slightly in Sydney's direction as though they were engrossed in conversation.

ოოო

Rosalind felt a smile tug at her mouth while she watched the men waiting for them. "They look pretty serious over there. What do you think they're plotting?"

"Heaven knows. Maybe the end of the world?" Syd offered. "But more likely the rodeo stats. Even though he can be as cosmopolitan as they come, Dev sure likes to watch people get crunched by a bull," she finished as they came up to the table.

Devin smiled up at his wife. "Nice to see the bull getting his own from time to time. Not like they get any other fun out of life. Their relatives get ground up for burgers and they're not even allowed to inseminate on their own."

"Unlike humans," Ty interjected. When three sets of

eyes turned his direction, he was busy waving to the waitress and indicating more coffee. Only then did he meet their gazes, innocently. "What? For the most part, humans inseminate naturally. Cattle've become big business. Couple of collections and you have a year's worth of baby calves—no muss, no fuss. No fun."

Sydney seemed more interested in the menu. "Isn't this a cheery conversation?"

Ty shrugged. "You get yourself involved with a couple of shit-kickin' cowboys, you gotta know you'll be talking insemination from time to time. If we were farmers, it would be crop rotation. Fact is, reproduction is as natural, and as critical, as pretty much anything going on in the world."

"And often going on far too often," Devin pointed out. "What's everyone want to eat? I'm starving. How about you, babe? Burger and fries sound good, or are you still on that health kick?" Sydney went pale, and Dev's teasing went to concern. "Hey, you okay?"

"Fine. If the soup's fresh, I'll have that. Or a chicken sandwich. Nothing fried."

"Your tummy giving you trouble again?"

"My stomach's fine." The words came out frosty.

Devon set down the menu to lean toward her. "You've been kind of urpy in the mornings lately. Sure you didn't pick up a bug in Florida? That place is a hotbed of disease."

"I'm fine," Sydney said, her teeth grinding audibly.

"No need to snap, Sydney. Dev's worried about you." Ty sounded suspiciously normal, but his expression was a bit too bland.

Sydney whipped her head in his direction, eyes narrowing. But Ty gave no indication he was interested in anything more important than what to have with his burger.

The waitress brought drinks—iced tea and more coffee for the women, beers for the men. Then she took the orders, assuring Sydney the soup was fresh and made with extra vegetables.

Talk became desultory while they waited, with Sydney avoiding Devin's eyes and Rosalind trying not to let on she knew anything about anything. Until Ty spoke up. "Seems Mosby's going to have some fun, come spring. He'll get some ladies visiting."

"You still won't ship semen?" Sydney asked, obviously grateful for the new conversational topic.

"Nah, too much research shows the more vital foals come from actual breedings. Plus he deserves a break. Not like he'll be any kind of a high-use stud."

"Isn't that more of an urban myth?" Rosalind asked. "I've done some research on this myself—for a book," she interjected, before they could degenerate into idiocy. "It's not proven one way or the other. And there is a certain amount of danger involved in natural breedings."

"Worth the risk. The Thoroughbred industry is still natural breedings, at least if you want to race." Ty took a sip from his fresh beer. "Seems some respected breeders felt that produced the best runners. Plus, it keeps the gene pool a little more open."

Devin grinned and grabbed a handful of nuts to go with his beer. "Well, some human gene pools might need a bit more chlorine in the shallow end."

Sydney's face was flushed, her eyes suspiciously bright. "You might think that's funny, but you are so wrong, buddy."

Finally sensing the undercurrents, Devin stopped, hand poised to toss the nuts into his mouth. His eyes widened as realization hit him head on. "Oh, shit. You're pregnant."

"Thus once again proving your sensitivity to the world." Sydney tried to push her chair back, but Devin hooked his foot under the leg, held it in place, and then pulled her closer.

Dropping the nuts on the table, he reached out to wrap his fingers around her arm. "How long have you known?"

"A couple weeks, maybe a month."

"When were you planning to tell me?" he asked, his question coming out in a growl.

"After this assignment. I would have told you at the ranch since it looked like we wouldn't be in the field. Then Maria came back and it looked more and more like Rosalind was going to get shafted."

His eyes darkened as he searched his memory. "That

last night, when I gave you a hard time about the chicken stew. That's why you didn't want me to make chili, the peppers were bothering you?"

She nodded, refusing to look away from the anger in his face.

"You didn't think, maybe, I should know before we went hauling ass out of there?"

"I'm pregnant, Devin. Not crippled. Pregnancy is a fact of life for women all over the world, not a disease. If it hadn't been for Mr. Big Mouth over there, you wouldn't have needed to know until this was over with."

"And how the hell did he know when I didn't?"

"Like I said," Ty chimed in. "Sometimes I pay attention. Besides, I grew up with two sisters and plenty of female cousins. Some of the signs are pretty obvious."

Devin aimed a narrow eyed glare at his friend. "Like?"

"Like tired and nauseous while the fetus is implanting in the womb. Strange food likes or dislikes," Rosalind joined in, and they all looked at her as if realizing she was still at the table. "More research, not personal experience. Not a lot of pregnancies among my coworkers, at least not the models. Borderline anorexia doesn't lend itself to easy propagation."

"Well, if Ty had kept his big mouth shut, we wouldn't be having this conversation," Syd grumbled.

Rosalind grinned. "I think at some point even Devin might have noticed. Eventually, there are some more obvious signs." She took a sip of her coffee, eyes sliding closed to better appreciate the flavor.

"I wasn't planning to keep it a secret forever, dammit. I was just—"

"Keeping it to yourself until you could come up with the best time to break it to me?" Devin drawled.

"Until we could get this one damned job over with so I could retire without worrying about someone I care about," she snapped, refusing to let the tears pooling in her eyes fall.

With a soft curse, Devin gathered her up in his lap. "Babe, I'm sorry. I'm acting like an ass here."

"You're not sorry I'm pregnant?"

"I'm not at all sorry we're going to have a baby. A little worried maybe since you are kind of puny after— oof!" Her small fist punched his arm. "Well, you are smaller than me."

"There are omnibuses smaller than you. I suppose your mother was six feet tall and three feet wide?"

He held her closer, ignoring the people around them. "Point taken."

"Now how do you feel about chlorine in the gene pool?" Danger edged through her quiet voice.

"Really depends on the genes. Yours, I don't mind seeing reproduced. Mine, I kind of wonder about."

"Not a lot of choice in that, buddy," Ty said quietly. "And I think you might want to put that part of yourself behind you. You're not your old man, and you'll do a hell of a lot better job raising your kids."

"Kids?" Devin paled even more. "Dammit, I'm just getting used to the idea of one of them." He stood, lowering Sydney gently to stand on her feet.

"I think we're going to want the food to go, if you don't mind," Rosalind said to the waitress approaching with their order.

"No problem. Is everything okay?"

"It's fine, thank you." Roz turned to Sydney. "We'll bring your food up when it's ready."

Devin nodded but didn't acknowledge them otherwise. Bending over to bring his head closer to the woman at his side, he ushered her out of the room.

Ty's eyes danced as he toasted his retreating partner. "Thus are the mighty fallen."

"That's not very nice."

"You didn't know Dev in the old days. He was one tough *hombre*. Still is for the most part, but he's purely soft about that little lady. Best thing ever happened to him."

"To both of them, it seems." Rosalind hoped she didn't sound as wistful as she felt.

"We need to get this figured out and done with so they can concentrate on growing a baby."

They grabbed the go bags, paid, and left.

❧❧❧

The meal ended up in Devin and Sydney's suite, with food spread across several surfaces. Sydney had her computer in her lap, on top of a pillow, while she stared at the screen. Her expression had gone from lively and involved to remote, and she barely looked up when chatter and enticing aromas filled the room.

"Babe, your soup's here."

She turned her attention to Devin with an obvious effort then looked over to Rosalind with a frown.

"What?" Rosalind asked, then she knew.

It had only been a matter of time.

Sydney looked at Devin then Ty.

Devin nodded. Both of them stood. "We'll mosey on out to the porch, soak up some rays."

"No need." Rosalind worked hard to keep her voice controlled. "Whatever she asks, you're going to find out anyway."

"I don't mind stepping out for a minute," Devin said.

"No," Ty said, his voice quiet. "If Roz wants me to stay, I'll stay."

"It might not be pretty," Sydney warned.

Rosalind's voice was threaded with steel. "Pretty is watching the sun go down behind the mountains, painting the snow in orange and gold. Pretty is seeing Mosby prance down the trail, pretending he doesn't know the first damned thing about reins or bit or leg aids, but still very careful of his rider."

When she paused, Ty moved from his position, frozen on the way to the glass door, to ease onto the couch next to her, his hand going from her shoulder to the back of her neck with a comforting stroke.

Taking strength from his support, she kept on. "I was kidnapped and left for dead. I'm apparently being chased around the country. I don't know why, for either event. Pretty has nothing to do with it. Everyone in this room will learn about what really happened sooner or later. I'd rather you heard from me." When Sydney still hesitated, Roz forced out the next words. "Just ask, okay?"

Sydney set her computer aside and slid onto the couch to the other side of Rosalind, reaching out to take her hand in a strong grip. She took a deep breath. "Roz, when you were there—when they kidnapped you—were you raped?"

Rosalind felt Ty's warm, hard, body next to her grow tense but his fingers never stopped their comforting caress on her neck—as if, no matter what she said, he was still there for her.

"I'm kind of surprised," she managed in the fake sophisticated voice she'd learned to use when she was overwhelmed by events. "I would have expected to be asked how many innocent young men I forced to sleep with me, due to my whorish behavior."

"There's been Internet noise about the Western woman who serviced a terrorist cell, but it's not gaining much momentum." Sydney's voice was matter of fact, as if they were discussing inventory quotas. "Seems no one wants to name names. Funny thing is, none of this came up until a few months ago."

Roz raised her head to meet her new friend's eyes, searching for any sort of accusation. She found none. "That's about when I got out of the camp?"

"More like when you moved back to your apartment in New York. Before that you were behind several layers of protection. But, Roz, you didn't answer me."

"Sorry. No, I wasn't raped." She could feel disbelief in the room and sighed. "I was not raped. Not for lack of trying. They had me down, several of them. On the ground with some campfires for light."

It all came rushing back, the lust on their faces, some holding her down, some shifting material to stroke themselves. The harsh feel of sand pushing into her back, then two of them grabbing her legs to pull them apart, no matter how hard she fought.

Ty's arm slid across her back, holding her close, and she felt him draw a shaky breath.

"What happened?" Syd managed to ask in an undertone.

By now Devin had moved onto the wide couch beside Syd and had his arm around her.

"I had my period." There. She said it. She revealed that which should never be uttered in public by any well-brought-up girl. She felt them all draw a deep breath. "Yep, Granny Grumps saved the day."

"They didn't, because—"

"Seems no matter how driven mad by my dangerously lustful behavior they were, those decent young men could not risk poisoning their precious boy bits."

They'd thrown her legs to the ground with bruising force, yelled at her, and kicked her, then tossed her into the dark room, slamming the door behind her, locking her in with the snap of a bar being dropped.

"So the whole time you were in that cell—nearly a week?" Sydney asked, even more gently.

"Not the whole week. Just added a soupcon of fun to the situation."

"Don't," Ty said with a barely controlled savage note in his voice. "Do not trivialize what happened to you."

"I have to, Ty. If I don't, then I'm not sure when I'll stop screaming." Roz stood, moving away from the comfort of his arm. Smoothed down her incredibly ugly jeans and managed a smile. "If you'll excuse me?"

Without waiting for a response, she headed to the bathroom. What was meant to be a casual stroll became anything but. Strong, measured steps followed behind her as she barely made it to the toilet.

ာၐၐ

Back in their room, locked in a bathroom with her own shampoo and scented cream, Rosalind tried to regain control. A shower helped, but no amount of soap and hot water completely eradicated the memory of those fingers grabbing at her breasts, or those hands holding her down. Now that she had allowed herself to remember, she couldn't make herself forget. Finally turning off the water, she dried her body and her pathetic hair, then pulled on the plush bathrobe. Drawing as deep a breath as she could manage, she turned off the light and stepped through the door.

Ty sat in one of the plush chairs, a bottle of water on the table next to him. The drapes were open to the valley below but the room remained shrouded in shadows. There was enough ambient light to see his ankle rested across his opposite knee, and he seemed to be contemplating the panoply of lights outside.

"I—I thought—" she began, meanwhile correcting her internal, *I was afraid*, which is what would have come out if she'd been more honest, at least with herself.

"You thought I was going to look for another room?"

She flung her hand out sideways, feeling helpless.

"Why can't you have more faith in me?" His soft voice came to her out of the shadows.

"Some lessons are hard to unlearn."

"I'm sure there's a lifetime of stories in there, but for now let's concentrate on what happened in that hell hole," he said, still with that soft voice that caressed her senses but now held a vein of heated steel. Ty was nowhere near as controlled as he was trying to appear.

"Somehow this makes it easier."

"How do you mean?"

She hadn't realized she'd said that out loud. "It's—when you're all controlled and calm, it's difficult to—because—"

Now he stood, a controlled release of energy and power. He stopped, close enough to touch but not raising his hand. She took a small step forward, then another one. Until she was in his arms, held safe against his chest.

"This is how it will be, Roz. As much as I can control, you will never again be coerced or held down or forced."

Finally, she broke.

$$e \cdot \mathfrak{I} e \cdot \mathfrak{I}$$

Eventually, she subsided into small hiccups and brief twitches of arms or legs. Ty had shifted them to the bed, pulling the covers over her to help protect her from any chill. He knew under the thick fluffy robe was bare silken skin but for once, he had very little desire to touch her.

She murmured, and he leaned in closer to hear. "Sorry."

He restrained the immediate flash of rage. So much for being the guy in control. "Nothing to be sorry for," he managed through a tight throat.

She swallowed then shifted, as though trying to move higher on the pillows. He helped, recognizing her need not to be on her back.

When she was propped against a mountain of soft

pillows, she accepted the bottle of water sitting on a side table.

After a few sips, she took a deep breath. "I never—" She hesitated. "I guess I lived a kind of charmed life. No great traumas, a mother who supported me any way she could, good friends, good teachers. So I was never challenged before. I thought I was so tough."

He held himself back from responding, sensing she needed to talk her way through this. His heart ached at the lost note in her voice. All that sass, all that indomitable force of will reduced to this shaking voice.

"No one had ever hit me, no one ever held me down, or even thought about forcing me to do anything. Now…" She shuddered.

He folded his hand over hers, holding as gently as he could.

She tensed, then her fingers curled slightly, as though to acknowledge the contact. "I kept—I kept pushing away everything after they carried me out. In the hospital, even at Stormhaven, I hid from it. It happened to someone else. But now I can't get rid of the feeling of their hands all over me. Then I think of women and girls around the world, abused, raped, no control over their lives, but they get up and keep going. The first time someone slapped me, I folded."

Acting on instinct, he bent over to press his lips against her wrist in a gossamer touch. After a moment, he felt her raise her other hand to touch his hair. He took that hand as well, nibbling along her arm as gently as he could manage. "No," he said in a low, intense voice. "They don't always get up and keep going. Especially not on their own in a completely foreign country with no idea what's going on."

"Look at Maria's sister, an abusive husband who treated her like a punching bag—"

He raised his head. "And it took him almost killing her and threatening her children, until she agreed to have him put in jail, and then make herself scarce when he was getting out. That's with the help of her neighbors, her friends, her sister, and this last time, Jamie for support. You were alone, Roz. Alone and scared and facing something completely out of your realm of knowledge." He rubbed his cheek along the soft inside of her forearm, relishing the tiny bumps raising on her skin. "When will you learn to have faith in yourself? You've done so much for others. I bet you were helping out those anorexic girls you worked with. Did you protect them from the two legged snakes?"

She shrugged, and he saw her tiny grimace, as though what she did was not so important.

"Before, when we…"

He stumbled into silence, but she knew what he was asking.

"I buried it. Same as I've always buried anything bad as long as it wouldn't hurt anyone else. Life needs to be about the good stuff."

"And we dug it out?"

"Kind of."

"Probably seemed like we were shoving you off the dock to make you swim." He exhaled on a bitten off curse. "Ah, Roz, I'm so sorry."

"You made me face it, which I needed to do if I was going to move on. Especially if I was going to help find out why."

He eased up her body, pushing aside the opening of the robe so he could taste and scent her neck. Her fingers still rested on his hair as if she needed to touch him. His fingertips stroked her skin, sliding underneath the thick robe, but stopped when she shuddered. "Too much?"

"What—what are you doing?"

"Well, I thought I was touching you, but if you have to ask, I'm obviously doing something wrong."

She raised her brows. "Why?"

Deep inside, he laughed at the return of her personality. "Because you're gorgeous? Because I love the feel of your skin against my fingers? Because—" He stopped as her expression became more remote. "Because I wanted to touch you where they did, to help you forget."

She drew a deep breath, let it out slowly while the expression in her eyes deepened. "In that case," she whispered. "They touched me all over and I would love for you to help me forget about them."

His fingers stilled while he looked for truth in her face. Then he inched his hand under the robe until his palm covered her breast and her nipple nudged into the middle of it.

She stilled, her luminous eyes staring into his while he held his breath. Then her arms raised to circle his neck and, with a quiet gasp, she turned to rest her head on his shoulder. Under the heated onslaught of his fingers, mouth, and breath, he felt those walls she'd built around her heart crack, crumble, and melt away.

Chapter 11

Nothing from Waters yet?" Ty asked the next morning as he passed around coffee refills.

Devin was stacking empty dishes from a hearty breakfast in Ty's suite.

"Not a damned thing, according to all the reports I've seen," said Sydney, scowling into her cup of tea. "It's like he dropped off the face of the earth."

"Not like Tony," Roz murmured. "Whatever else he's done this time, in the past, he always wanted to make an impact wherever he went."

Sydney looked up. "Not much of a wallflower?"

"Not even. He prefers behind the camera to in front, but he's not a shrinking violet. If he were involved in something, and I'm not saying he is, it's not in his nature to stay behind the scenes pulling strings. Much more like him to be leading the charge."

"If he can," Ty noted.

"Yeah, there is that. Any more news from Powers?" Roz kept her question intentionally impersonal.

"Not so far today but it's early yet for him." Sydney looked over, all attention on Roz. "He tends to be up late then sleep in a bit."

"So no idea when they're going to release my computer?"

Sidney frowned. "Okay, what's the big deal about your computer? You said you upload your files to an online account while you're working on them. What's on your computer that you need so badly?"

Roz hesitated then held up a small ring of keys and ornamental fobs.

Devin straightened. "Where'd you get that?"

"It usually stays either in my pocket or around my neck. It was in the pocket of that robe I was wearing on the raid and stayed with me in the hospital." She sorted through the various ornaments and indicated a tiny oblong shape.

In the ensuing silence, they could hear a lawn mower outside. Finally, Ty asked, "Is that a flash drive?"

Rosalind nodded. "I need my computer to read it."

"Sydney has pretty much every program known to man on her computer. Let's bring it down and we can have a look." Devin suggested, with a quick glance at his wife.

"I don't think she has this one," Rosalind cautioned.

"It's a private program a friend designed for me to hide files."

Sydney almost managed to suppress her obvious interest in the problem. "You don't upload that file?"

"This is the only copy. If anything happened to me, it wouldn't matter to anyone else."

Ty stared at the tiny drive then back at Rosalind Did he realize how much trust she placed in them, to reveal this last secret?

Looking away from the hesitation she knew was in her eyes for a brief second, he glanced at Sydney. "Tell Powers to stop dicking around with Rosalind's computer and get it over here. Yesterday."

Sydney nodded, reached for her phone, and rose to head for the balcony, dialing as she went.

Satisfied his message was being delivered, he turned back to Rosalind, mouth relaxing into a smile. "You want some of these pastries? Even with Syd on his butt it will take Powers a bit of time to get his rear in gear."

She opened her mouth. Closed it. No words wanted to form and fall out.

"What? It's a simple question. Pastries? No pastries?"

She shook her head, hard enough to knock loose some sense. "You're not going to grill me about what's on the drive or jump me for not trusting you sooner?"

"Way I look at it, neither one of us has been real forthcoming." He chose a pastry covered in slivered almonds and set it on a napkin. "We both have reasons to think we can't trust each other. Yours are probably light years harder than mine to overcome. I figure—" He lifted the coffee pot, raised an eyebrow, then shrugged when she shook her head. "Way I figure is you'd tell me when you thought I needed to know."

"Not hearing this." Devin went to join Sydney.

Ty moved back to the chair across from her. "Now, in my mind, you should have needed to tell me maybe in Florida or at least a couple nights ago."

She wavered between outrage and amusement. "So, in your mind, sleeping with you means I can automatically trust you with my secrets?"

"Ouch. Put it that way…well, yeah. It's pretty obvious you don't sleep around. So sleeping with me, letting yourself be at risk emotionally, was a biggie for you. Seems like the trust would go a little deeper."

"It's not the same."

He shrugged, biting into the pastry. Flakes of fresh crust broke off to settle on his lips. "Yeah, it can be harder to let the emotions go for some people."

"You haven't exactly been monogamous your whole adult life, have you?"

"Hell, no. Except when I was married. Once we said those vows, I stuck to them, temptation or not."

"For which, of course, you expect a gold star on both butt cheeks."

He opened his mouth to retort then grinned. "Almost

got me on that one but you're not changing the subject. It's different for a guy."

She nodded, pretending to accept his statement. "Of course it is. You have a tab, women have a slot. Big difference. What makes you think there should be less emotional involvement for a man than for a woman?"

"When did I say that?"

"Think back about two sentences. 'It's different for a guy'?"

"Well, yeah." His voice and expression showed nothing but conviction. "Very few guys go on a date thinking wedding bells and fancy white dresses. Much less the key to unlock the secret garden."

"You think that's all a woman has on her mind? And excuse me, where did this secret garden crap come from?"

His grin was pure devilment. "Thought that one would get you." He took a sip of coffee.

"So now you're picking an argument to distract me?"

"Pisses you off, doesn't it?"

"More like makes me wonder what we're doing here."

"Trying to communicate, sweetheart."

"Please don't use casual endearments. I'm sure they work most of the time, but I really don't like being lumped with every woman you've ever slept with."

His confused look would have been endearing if she wasn't on her way to a good mad.

"It's not a casual endearment."

"No? Then why did you sit down over there?" She kept her tone low and even, though she was ready to curl up into herself. Damned insecurities.

He finally saw the worry she was trying not to show in her eyes, the tension in her hands. "You waiting for me to rain all over you for not immediately trusting me? You'll have to wait a little longer, cupcake. And, as far as where I'm sitting—"

He paused and deliberately looked her up and down, letting her see the heat in his eyes. When he spoke this time, his voice was little more than a rough whisper, caressing her ears the way his work-hardened hands had caressed her skin. "If my partner and his wife weren't fifteen feet away and we weren't expecting a knock on the door any second now, you wouldn't be alone on that couch." He measured the length of the couch with a practiced eye. "Hell, you wouldn't be on that damned couch at all, it's too short for what I have in mind."

"What's that?"

"About an hour of me tasting every luscious inch of you. Then another hour or so of you doing the same with me. Followed by the rest of the night with me inside you one way or another."

She jerked upright, meeting his gaze. Those brilliant blue-green eyes were sharp with possession, and memories of the night before. She glanced down at his lap, and lifted her lips in a secret female smile.

He chuckled. "Yeah, you grin all you want. You'll be walking bowlegged by the time I'm done with you."

"Promises, promises."

Whatever else she was going to say, and she really wasn't sure what it would be, was cut off by a firm knock on the door. Ty started to stand, then sank down, readjusting his jeans carefully as he did.

"You want me to go to the door?" she asked with a small evil smile.

"Might not be a good idea, depending on who's out there. I'm thinking Dev and Sydney—yep."

Devin passed them on his way to the door, glancing at Ty and smirking. Sydney followed, stepping to the opposite side of the door.

"Who is it?" Devin barked out.

The answer came in a mumble and he looked at Sydney who nodded once. "I'm going to open the door. Show me." Devin opened the door enough for a hand to enter, holding a laptop computer with dinosaur stickers randomly decorating the cover.

Sydney looked over at Roz. "Dinosaurs?"

"Great distraction when you're around people who think the world is only six thousand years old. It also makes it difficult for someone to replace the laptop without me knowing."

Devin shook his head, maintaining his standard grim expression for the people on the other side of the door, but Sydney could flash a grin. While Devin held the laptop, Sydney raised her eyebrows and spoke to the people on the other side of the door. "Cord. Now."

After a moment the protective case and charging cord came through the door, which was then closed and locked. Roz came over to reach for her laptop, holding it against her chest while she diverted to Sydney, who had leaned back against the wall.

"You all right?"

"Feeling a little ragged. Strange for me."

"Hormones'll do that to you every time. And no, this is not permission for either one of you guys to blame hormones for anything."

The males both made the classic "not me, boss" gestures. Devin looked between the two women and raised his eyebrow but didn't say anything.

Doing a poor job of hiding her smirk, Rosalind set her laptop up on the table. "How did you get Powers to move?"

"Now that it might hold a clue, he had no trouble returning your property and didn't understand why you didn't have it already."

"Amazing."

"That's one way of looking at it. I was thinking more along the lines of how could they expect you to cooperate if they won't work with you."

"And this is your boss?"

"No one is her boss," Devin interjected.

Roz gave a mock clap with her hands before turning

back to her laptop. "Ooh, high score on this round of dealing with the opposite sex to the big guy in old jeans for getting in a zinger without prompting."

"Very funny, Roz," Devin said. "And how is your particular battle of the sexes coming along?"

"No battle. No sex. No problem." Ty kept his voice intentionally bland.

Devin gave a short bark of laughter, not fooled by his partner's crossed-leg position on the couch.

Cord plugged in, laptop charging, Roz started it up then, once it was humming along, she inserted the minuscule flash drive. The screen filled with incomprehensible symbols, and their collective shoulders drooped. Rosalind's fingers danced over the keys.

All of them looked at her in surprise.

"You never said you could coax computers." Sydney sounded almost offended

"Mostly just my baby here. We've been together for such a long time." She leaned forward, accessing drives and pulling up files. "Damned ham-handed hackers think they know how to access files. They insulted the baby. Now we have to talk very nice to her. There you go, baby." She stroked a few more keys, and the symbols resolved into words.

Ty leaned over her shoulder, focused on the screen, and she allowed herself a discreet enjoyment of his proximity. "Another manuscript?"

She nodded briskly. "Got it in one."

While the file assembled itself, Roz jumped to an-other screen and brought up an e-mail program.

Sydney leaned forward. "You do know Powers has been tracking your e-mail, don't you?"

"I doubt he's found this program. It's kind of ob-scure and I rarely use it."

"You don't access your e-mail on your phone?"

Roz raised one eyebrow, looking over with a pained expression. "I use my phone to make phone calls and, if it's critically necessary, I'll send a text. Besides which, my phone, with all the contacts, was left in an elevator ceiling in Florida."

"Right. We should get those back for you." Sydney promised.

Roz shrugged. "Other than the phone numbers and maybe a few photos, it really doesn't matter much. I don't store information on my—" Then she grunted. "What's this?" She leaned closer to the screen, scrolling through the website "Tony asked if he could use my computer when he visited the ranch," she muttered. "Huh, wonder what that's all about?" She settled back in her chair, looked around. "What do you know about Stone Mountain?"

 cɔɛɔ

An hour or so later, they presented the same question to Powers.

"It's a theme park in Georgia, east of Atlanta. It has rides and other attractions. The main draw is a mountain carving," Powers said, stirring his tea.

"Like Rushmore?" Ty asked.

"Yes, except this is of Lee, Jackson, and Davis."

At their continued blank stares, Powers sighed and went on, "Robert E. Lee, Stonewall Jackson, and Jefferson Davis. It's a tribute to the leaders of the Confederate Army."

"Bingo, boys and girls," Rosalind spoke up. "If Tony really is involved, I think I know what this is all about. After I stopped modeling and went into full time writing, there was a time when we didn't see much of each other. Tony took some assignments in the South, said he wanted to get back to his roots, kidding about the TV movie. He did some fashion shoots but spent time traveling around, stopping wherever he pleased and taking lots of pictures. Some great stuff." Rosalind took a sip of water, then rolled the glass between her hands, watching the concentric circles forming on the table from the damp base. She shook her head, clearing out her thoughts.

"We didn't see much of each other and didn't communicate much. We've never been much for weekly phone calls or daily e-mails. One or the other of us would call from time to time, do an info dump, then nothing for months. It worked for us."

She rose to pace around the room, avoiding everybody's gaze. Staring out the window, she was careful to stand well away from the sheer curtains. "Then I got a call in the middle of the night. Tony was euphoric about someone he met. 'He could very well be the one,' was what he said. He described him as smart, funny, and, of course, gorgeous, though our definitions of gorgeous tended to differ. They met in a small town in Georgia and spent the next few weeks touring other small towns, old farms, and antique auctions, anything 'quaint and cute' Tony could photograph. He had—has—a way of making the most commonplace location look spectacular."

She ran a hand through her short hair, continuing to face the window. "We probably talked for...oh, half an hour or so, with me mostly incoherent since I only got a few hours of sleep those nights while trying to meet a deadline. He promised to get back to me with more information, but his new squeeze was coming into the room and I'd lost his attention."

Now she turned and came back to lean on the back of her chair. "He didn't call back. Next I heard, his agent was calling me to find out if I knew where he was. Seems he'd dropped out of sight."

Ty moved to stand near her. "Like now."

"I hope not. I was done with my rough draft by then, so I took a trip down to Georgia, to the last place he'd been, right outside Atlanta. Oxford, a cute little town—they held the equestrian events there for the Georgia Olympics. He dropped enough small town names I was eventually able to follow his trail. Tracked him back to

Atlanta, to Grady Memorial, where they treat unknown trauma victims. He spent a week in a coma. He was found without any ID and apparently no one was looking real hard for it. Seems they didn't take too kindly to faggot black artists down here in good-ol'-boy country."

Ty touched the small of her back. She managed a tight smile. "He was starting to come around and, once they knew he had insurance, they took him out of the public ward and put him in a private room. Even paid a little more attention to him. It didn't do any good, once he woke up, since no one would listen to him. He'd been found alone, but when he was jumped, he was with his new friend.

"When the sheriff's deputies found him down a hill on the side of the road he was still somewhat conscious, and he kept telling them there was someone else. They ignored him. After I arrived, we got the state police involved, and they took out the tracking dogs. They found Tony's friend in about an hour, maybe half a mile away from where they found Tony. If they cared to look sooner..." Her mouth tightened and she shook her head.

"Once Tony was ready to travel, we busted the hell out of that place and went back to New York. For some strange reason, his cameras and all his equipment escaped unscathed, still locked in the trunk of his rental car that mysteriously lost both foot and emergency brakes before rolling down a hill. The pictures were amazing, especially the ones of his new friend."

"And you're just telling us about this now, because?" Powers's voice carried a deceptively mild tone.

Giving him her best haughty look, Rosalind answered, "For one thing, it was nearly ten years ago. For another, until I heard what Stone Mountain meant, I had no idea why or how he could be involved. Tony stopped talking about what happened, about getting even with what he called the asshole pricks with billy clubs, a year or so after we came back to New York. I know he was seeing a therapist and got his life back on track."

She stepped away from Ty and glared at Powers. "You're the one with the cracker-jack research teams. Why didn't they uncover any of this? I'm sure you had them digging into all our lives down to the most minute speck of dust on our first ponies."

Powers didn't even flinch. "Perhaps not that far, but we had what I thought were comprehensive files. I will certainly be looking into this oversight. In the meantime, why would you connect this unfortunate incident with recent occurrences?"

She didn't bother hiding her snarl. "Because the retrograde knuckle draggers who killed his friend and left Tony for dead were all about the past and future glory of the South and how they knew how to treat blackies back then. Wouldn't ever let them get uppity or dye their hair pink and purple or wear fancy clothes. Tony never did understand the idea behind conservative. With him, what you saw was what you got."

"Bringing us back to him involving you," Powers pointed out.

Rosalind moved back to the table, Ty shadowing her. "That's where you lose me. Tony wouldn't involve me, especially if he was out to get even here. He understands the whole idea of revenge as a dish best served cold, but he also understands loyalty." She looked around the room, feeling like she needed them to understand what she knew instinctively. "When he finally woke in the hospital and first saw me, he grinned with his broken teeth and split lips, and told me he knew I'd be the one to track him down and come to help. He would never betray that sort of trust."

"Could he possibly have involved you inadvertently?" Powers suggested.

"Maybe, but it would be really convoluted. Wait." She sank into her chair then dropped her face into her hands, her elbows on the table. "If that website was left on my computer to give me a hint of what might be happening—" She raised her head. "Oh my God, I think I figured it out.

"Tony introduced me to Hamad. He knew I was looking for an in to the real Middle East, not just the accepted or approved tourist areas. He met Hamad at a horse sale somewhere, where he did a shoot for the some of the ranches. Got to know him pretty well and figured I'd jump at the chance. Of course he was right. For his part, Hamad seemed to enjoy my company and saw me as a way he to get his family to back off. I guess Tony shared a bit of our background in an attempt to get me an invitation." She narrowed her eyes, shutting out the others as much as possible to dig into her memory. "Then, one day while we were talking—Hamad and Raheem and one or two others—about prejudice and unfair treatment, I told them about Tony's experiences in Georgia." She looked down. "The raid was a few days later."

"Do you think that could be the connection?" Sydney suggested.

"Connection to what? Mind if I'm included in information about my life and future?"

"We know some of Raheem's friends have snuck into the country," Powers said. "We know they're in the South. We suspect they're behind the bomb in your room in Florida, but we're not positive. The elderly-seeming couple you saw was a team from a domestic agency."

"Are they really that incompetent or just good actors?"

"Not important at this point."

"They must be *really* incompetent," Devin muttered to Ty in an intentionally loud voice, before giving Powers an innocent face.

"So I'm an immediate suspect because I was in the Middle East?"

"That, your association with Hamad, plus a story they couldn't verify, and your disappearance."

"What story? Who couldn't verify? If I wasn't there,

how could I disappear? Are you going to tell me who my savior was—who called you about my disappearance from somewhere I'd never visited?"

"It's scary, but I actually understood that." Ty rubbed her shoulder, and she offered a slight smile.

Powers pulled a slim folder out from his briefcase. "A truly anonymous call, from a female in the town you visited. She gave enough details and fortunately found the right person at the US Embassy, so there wasn't as big of a delay as there could have been. Once we knew the general area, it only took an extra day to find the approximate location of the compound."

"How did all that carnage, all those bodies, get explained away?"

"There were no bodies to explain, at least not when you were removed. No carnage, except for the dead goats attracting buzzards and flies. No loss of life. Raheem wasn't precisely lying when he said it was a game. He neglected to tell you who the actual victim of the game was." He reached into his pocket for a pipe, began the tedious task of packing and lighting, then looked up. "You."

"Why?" She tried hard not let her frustration and confusion show.

"Discredit the American, take down the female who dared to walk around turning the heads of good men," Devin suggested. "Who understands the mind of a zealot?"

"I can't say 'he seemed so normal' since he always seemed to be on edge and ready to attack someone. He was always spouting the Koran and getting it wrong. More research," she explained quickly. "But it is a beautiful piece of writing."

"When it's not used to justify a holy war," Powers reminded her.

"Like no one's ever done that with the Bible?"

"Point taken, Ms. Summerton."

She interlaced her fingers, clenching against the need to do something. "Question still is, why now?"

A large, rough hand settled over hers, holding and comforting. Ty leaned forward, shutting out the rest of the room. "Roz, when did you talk about Tony to Hamad and his friends?"

"At Baheera's home. The same time I took those pictures." She saw a question in his face but at first couldn't understand what he needed to know.

"When did they plan this mock raid?"

"The next day…" She trailed off, mind racing. "Do you think they saw Tony's history as a way to manipulate him?"

"I think the timing of what they heard and what they did to you is a too much of a coincidence." He squeezed lightly, and she turned her hand to slide her palm against his. "It's also possible they thought they might use you to control Tony," he continued. "Except that anonymous woman called in an alert, and someone pulled the media card from your camera to make sure we got those pictures."

Sydney nodded. "It could have been a matter of convenience, or maybe circumstances being in their favor. They saw an advantage and grabbed it."

"So Hamad never really wanted me to meet his parents?" Roz then shook her head. "No, that's not right. Up until that party, he was or seemed sincere. And I didn't see him after the raid."

Sydney spoke up, her attention on the computer screen in front of her. "Could this all have been an elaborate ruse on the part of Hamad and/or Raheem, and company, to find a patsy for whatever attack they were planning?"

Devin grinned. "Married me a smart one here, didn't I?"

She popped him in the upper arm, and he feigned a flinch.

Powers set his pipe aside and leaned forward. "What makes you say that?"

"Hearing Rosalind tell it, it's obvious this Tony cares about her. Enough so, he introduces her to someone who can help her with the research. Everything was hunky do-ry in the Middle East until they met Mansur, then Raheem started acting strange, less friendly or tolerant of Roz. I'm betting they proposed this fake raid as a way for you to get some hands-on experience with life as a Bedouin raider?" At Rosalind's nod, she gave a tight smile and went on. "So they have you set up in a raid where you see people killed and I'm betting they planned to use that as blackmail, or as a lever with Tony. You were stuck in that old compound, but someone tried to rescue you—we can't be sure who it was. There are so many rebel factions and ultra-conservative radicals over there, it's pretty hard without a scorecard to tell who is who, and that only holds true for one day. When those raiders didn't find you, the story went out you were never there. Hamad was reported as being at home and happy after attending the important horse show. He even came back with a horse." She looked over at Roz for confirmation.

"A couple horses, actually. Nice ones."

Powers muttered something that sounded suspiciously like, "Damned horse people."

The rest of the people in the room chose to ignore him.

"I'm following so far," Rosalind said slowly. "When I wasn't found at the compound or whoever came to the compound couldn't brag about finding me, they changed their plans. But where does Tony fit in?"

"If he was in on it with them from the beginning, then he's not the good friend you believed in," Sydney pointed out. "What if they decided to use Tony's past to convince him he could get even with the people who hurt his lover, when they couldn't use you as a lever. Maybe they convinced him to go with them from the airport, when he came back from the ranch. Good chance they didn't know where he was, since the tickets to Denver were picked up at the last minute and he pretty much dashed off."

"Do you think he threw in with them?" Roz asked in a flat tone.

"Roz," Ty murmured.

"It's okay, the sooner I know, the easier it will be to put it behind me."

"That one's harder to be sure about." Syd studied her computer screen. "I'm looking up what happened eight years ago, but it didn't get a lot of press. Looks like the deputies involved got a slap on the wrist and stayed on the force. Most of them anyway. One got bumped from the force later for other infractions and is a security guard at Stone Mountain."

They exchanged grim glances.

Devin took a sip of coffee, then reached for the carafe. "Think we can get someone to believe us?"

Ty held out his cup for a refill. "That a bunch of radical middle eastern dilettantes and a purple haired—or is it gold now?—photographer are planning a terrorist incident at Stone Mountain?"

"When you put it that way, even I would wonder," Rosalind admitted. "I still can't see Tony ever thinking about hurting anyone not directly implicated in his friend's death. Not the person I knew. Make the no-necks look bad, absolutely. Hurt kids and tourists? He might diss their clothes and take embarrassing pictures, but he couldn't hurt them."

"We're going to present this to the Georgia CID." Powers frowned. "Carter knows some people there." His assistant stepped forward at the use of his name. "If they accept the story, we can leave it in their hands."

"If they don't?" Rosalind kept her voice and expression level, professional.

"We'll have to take care of it ourselves. Either way, Ms. Summerton, I think it would be a good idea for you not to be here."

At this she tossed back her head, going for a diva effect. "I'm supposed to go sit in a corner and knit while my friend might be in trouble? If he is involved, I want to be there to smack him around myself."

"At the moment, you have several agencies still looking for you, and it's not in our best interest to let anyone know the truth. It might alert the terrorists."

Rosalind moaned. "Blonde wig and baggy jeans again?"

Powers gathered his folders and prepared to stand. "Unless you can come up with something more appropriate."

Ty moved back his chair, reaching to help Rosalind. "Who's going to look for Tony?"

"We won't forget about him," Powers promised.

❧❦❧

"Why do I feel like he patted me on the head and told me to run along like a good little girl?" Rosalind grumbled to Ty.

"Because, essentially, he did. Notice he did the same with the rest of us?"

"Yeah, why does he dismiss his own people?"

"We're too involved. Powers wants people with as little emotional involvement as possible. Says emotions are messy and unnecessary."

Ty looked around, left eyebrow raised. "You do know what this means?"

Sydney nodded. "Means we aren't working for or with Powers so there's no reason we can't hunt for Tony ourselves."

"That sneaky so and so." Roz almost smiled. "If that's the case, I've been thinking about that message I got, saying Sandy was in the hospital."

"The message no one else can find?" Sydney teased, stepping back from Roz's mock scowl. "What about it?"

"Tony is one of the few people who knows that would get me on a plane faster than anything. Well, unless he told me he was hurt himself. Still, that message got me to Florida."

"Why Florida?"

"I'm not sure. But what if they were pressuring him to get me out from wherever I was hiding and he decides to use that message to send me to the wrong place? Using my computer to research Stone Mountain left a honking

big clue, which would have shortcut a lot of effort if..."
She looked around meaningfully. "...said computer had
been available for my use."

"I wonder what we would see if we checked the
cameras at Hartsfield airport in Atlanta on the same day
you landed in Florida?" As she spoke, Sydney reached
for her computer. She dragged it closer, then asked as
casually as possible, "When are you going to share
what's on that flash drive?"

Roz hesitated then offered a small smile. "It's mostly
gibberish, I just needed access to that e-mail program
plus the password." She looked down as though embarrassed. "I suck at remembering passwords so I have them
all stored on the computer. I think Tony and I are about
the only people who use that program."

"There were a lot of words to be hiding an e-mail
program. I'm also wondering why Powers's people didn't
find that program. It can't be that obscure."

"The gibberish is a manuscript I've been kicking
around. Different from what I usually write."

Sydney lifted her eyebrows. "You store it only on the
flash drive?"

"Pretty much, especially if I have to go on the Internet."

"What kind of manuscript are you working on that
you need to keep so private?"

Roz visibly hesitated. "It's sort of a journal, but not
really. I was working on a book based on my experiences,

structured as the main character's journal. So it's about traveling in the Middle East, meeting Hamad at the horse show, and going with him to his family home. Impressions of his family and friends. Including going on that raid and ending up in the compound."

"You didn't have anything to write with there, did you?" Ty pointed out.

Roz smiled. "Yes, I did. I also have a pretty good memory for stories even if I suck at passwords. I keep the flash drive with me, so no one has seen what I've written."

"Is there anything in there we could use to figure out what the target might be?"

"It's possible. Now that I have the computer back, I was going to go through it tonight."

"Would two sets of eyes be better?" Ty's voice was quiet.

She hesitated then slowly nodded, as if making a great decision. "That would probably make the search go faster."

"What about four sets?" Sydney asked. "Can you save it in a standard format? Or would you rather not?"

This time her hesitation was longer. It was easy to see her fears mounting. Sydney gave her a small smile. "I know it's very personal. Anything we read stays with us, unless you decide it needs to go forward." She held out a slender flash drive.

After a minute, Rosalind accepted the drive then occupied herself with converting the file on her computer, saving it to the new drive, then erasing it from her computer. "Once you've read this—"

"I'll erase it with FileShredder, no problem. And I won't save it on my computer, nor go on line while it's open."

"Thank you." Simple words. Heartfelt emotions, expressing faith and trust.

Chapter 12

Ty didn't know what he expected from Rosalind's mock journal. The character was her, but it wasn't. She created a heroine from a Victorian/very early twentieth-century society lady, sophisticated and flighty, but with a good heart. Although extremely intelligent, she made some really dumb choices and was paying for them. The journal started in the prison, went back to first meeting Hamad, then—in detail—told about his family, his contacts, and his strange friends who wanted to stop all progress in their country, since automobiles and airplanes were not in the Koran. Most of all they wanted to hurt the infidel Christians who thought money solved all problems.

As her character pointed out, they weren't averse to

having their own money, just to earning it. Nor did they mind American music or clothes, just mocked them, deriding the people who wore those revealing clothes. It was all very confusing for the party girl now stuck in a hell hole somewhere in the middle of nowhere.

Sometime later he looked up. "You wrote all of this after your rescue?"

"No, I arranged it that way. I had one of those tiny computers with me and wrote most of it as it happened. Keeping a journal became a habit when I trained horses. That way, I never had to rely on my memory about what horse stumbled on Tuesday, or when we actually got a load of hay. It carried over when I started modeling, then I finally realized I'd rather be writing, especially when I ended up doing character sketches in the middle of my fashion comments."

The personal insight drew him into the story. Rosalind didn't stint on words or research. Every visit was described, right down to what the people wore and how they spoke. Her impressions of people were clear and concise. It seemed as if he were in the room with her. "Why haven't you had this published?"

"My agent got hold of a small part of it and is prepared to send it out for bid. She thinks it could be my breakout book."

Ty didn't completely understand the terminology but he could catch up on that later. "But you're not ready?"

"Not yet. Soon maybe. I wasn't ready before I came

to New Mexico, but at least there I could write on it without suffocating again."

"That's why you had to stay up all night, and the small windows bothered you."

"I never knew when someone was coming unless they shuffled their feet. Fortunately, they were all pretty lazy walkers."

"Who? The people walking up behind you when you were with Hamad?"

She twisted her pretty mouth in a grimace. "Raheem used to think it was funny to sneak up behind me and pull my hair at parties and when we were all sitting around. Said it was all in good fun."

He looked at her fashionably short haircut, and nodded in understanding.

She ran her long fingers along the side of her head, lifting what hair there was. "I cut my hair before the raid ruined what was left so this isn't totally because of him. In fact, if it had only been that, I would have worn it long just to prove he wasn't going to have any effect on my life."

He grinned "You are a stubborn wench, aren't you?"

"It's like working with a stallion. You can't out muscle them so you have to out think them. You never give them an inch, or they'll walk all over you."

"Words of wisdom from a really smart lady." He went back to studying the screen.

"You trying to sweet talk me, cowboy?"

"Is it working?"

"Might be. Might even be you could talk me into something more interesting once I get through this pile of words."

"I'm more interested in getting you out of something." His hand slid around her shoulder, and into the collar of her prim shirtwaist blouse. He eased his fingers under her bra strap, then one long calloused finger slid into the bra cup.

"Just let me. Oh, damn—" She shuddered as his fingers touched her nipple. "I have to close this down and take it off the hard drive." Her fingers danced, her body shuddered, and her breath caught. She barely managed to remove the flash drive and shut down the computer. "That's not fair."

"Not much is. But what were you talking about specifically?"

"The way you can distract me. It's never happened before."

A few days earlier, her blunt talk would have surprised him. But now, he knew this direct woman was the real Rosalind. Not the polite, friendly woman he first met at the ranch, but this slightly bawdy, slightly shy, call-a-spade-a-spade, woman, who, right now, was going glassy-eyed at the simple stroke of a finger over her nipple.

"Nice to know I can have this effect on you. God knows, you get my heart racing every time you walk across the room. Or cross your legs. Or, hell, every time you draw a breath. It's all I can do not to strip you down right there and climb on top of you. Or have you climb on top of me. I'm pretty flexible that way."

"I wouldn't think you'd be much for women on top."

"There you go, you went and woke up the little head."

Smiling that tiny feminine smile, she glanced over at the bulge in his jeans. Sure enough, the bulge twitched. On impulse, she leaned over to rest her cheek against his erection. Even through the heavy denim she could feel it throb.

Ty blew out a breath, trying hard for control. "You're living dangerously. I'm planning to get you into bed. You don't want to be sleeping out here on the floor."

She rubbed her cheek against him, all but purring. "You'd kick me out of your bed for wanting to rub you and wondering how you tasted?"

"Dammit, woman, I'm trying to be considerate here. You keep that up and we'll never get away from this table. I've been having fantasies about bending you over a table since the first time I saw your butt sticking up in the air."

"Hmmm. Well, my butt's not sticking up. But something else seems to be." She lifted her hand to shape his bulge, then reached for the button on his jeans.

"That damned toy done for the night?"

"Hmmm? Oh, yeah. Why?"

"Lock it up and take a good hold."

When she did, he lifted her and the laptop. "I figure if I can keep your hands full for a minute, we might get into the bedroom together. Just in case, I'd rather have the computer with us than in another room."

Once in the bedroom, he stopped by the armchair so she could set down the laptop, then he eased her down on the bed. He toed off his boots, while he pulled off her shoes. "Now where were we? Oh, yeah." His nimble fingers went to work on the buttons, then he laid open her blouse, exposing her bra. "How many of these damned things do you have, in how many colors?"

"I could have a lifetime supply, if I want, from several of the designers I modeled for. Any style I want, and in every color. I just don't always wear them."

"It's all lace and fluff. Damn, woman, if I'd known you were wearing something like this, you wouldn't have made it into that meeting."

"Think about this—I could be wearing one at any time. Or I could be wearing something white and plain. Or—" She writhed under the stroke of his fingers. "—I could be wearing nothing at all."

He sought the clasp, found it between her breasts, and loosened the ice blue bra, letting it fall open while he leaned down to trace the edges with his lips, then with his tongue. He nudged aside the pretty colored lacy thing to find and feast on her nipple.

Rosalind cried out, arching up to his active tongue,

sinking her fingers into his hair to pull him closer, her body in constant motion to press up against his, frantic for fulfillment.

Ty lifted his head far enough to let his lips keep stroking her nipple while he murmured. "Damn, woman, you are easy. How come no one ever figured that out before?"

"Maybe…" She ran her hands down his back, around his waist band, and sought the fastening on his jeans. "Maybe they weren't you. Where's the damned zipper?"

"Figured that might end up a dangerous idea and went with the classics. Ahhh."

Her fingers took on a life of their own, grabbing and pulling at buttons, until he reached down to help. Finally, finally he sprang free, eager for her touch. A quick tug made short work of the snaps on his western style shirt.

Her cool, long, graceful fingers slid around him, reaching down to cup him while she looked up. Her eyes—luminous, large, lavender fringed with dark— stared into his. She stroked, squeezed gently, claiming him for her own. When he could stand no more, he pushed his jeans down the rest of the way then reached for the fastening on her baggy slacks.

Lifting her up, he slid the slacks down her legs then completely off. He released the suction on her breast to look at her. Matching blue froth covered that most secret part of her. Shrugging out of his jeans, he stretched out beside her, leaning on his elbow, watching his large dark hand invade her creamy white skin, then slide under the pretty blue to settle between her legs, stroking, teasing. She parted her thighs, holding her breath as he inched one finger under the silk and lace.

"Look at this, sweetie." With his other hand he encouraged her to lift up on her elbows, to look down at his invasion. "You're all silk and cream and soft and girly. I'm all dark and rough." His hand pulled out from the side, disappeared down the front and showed ice blue lace and silk from the knuckles down. "Now I'm wearing your fancy undies and you—" His fingers dove, sought. "—you're wearing me."

Rosalind bucked, pushed, found a modicum of satisfaction. He laid her back down across his arm, reaching from behind to claim one breast while he leaned down to rest his mouth against the other one. She clutched at his head, ran her hands under his shirt, dug into his back. Pulled at his shoulder.

"Is this what you want, sweetheart?" Deliberately, he settled on her body, feeling her satiny breast against his chest, her nipples rubbing against his like points of fire. "Your nubs feel like fire on me. Come closer. Oh, yeah, I can almost understand wearing silk underwear." He slid his hand around to hold her bottom and rubbed himself between her legs, feeling the silk and lace caress him. Feeling the moisture seeping through.

Her hands slipped down, pushing at her underwear. "Want it gone. Just you and me."

He lifted off long enough to push away the offending material, to cover himself for her protection, then settled again. "Now that's what I'm talking about. Lift your knees, babe. Oh, yeah."

"Do you always talk so much during sex?" she panted as she wiggled and pushed against, him, trying desperately to get him there. Right there. Almost.

"I don't want to be a faceless voiceless hand in the dark. You're going to know who's with you and whose— oh, yeah." He fell silent as he sank into her, sheathing himself as deeply as he could, then lifted her up to meet his thrust.

Then the slow dance to soft music became a frantic be-bop of thrusting and writhing, of reaching out and taking hold. Of yielding and claiming. Of love.

Later, as they lay entwined, snuggled together as one beneath the covers, she thought to ask. "Did you see anything I might have missed in the journal?"

"Might be. But we don't need to talk about it tonight. You snuggle up right there, and let me hold you while we sleep."

Safe within each other's arms, they slept.

∽∾∽

The next morning they met in the other suite. Sydney poured out coffee while she talked. "We went through the journal fast, then went back page by page, and found what might be significant references. I don't know if you remember them since it looks like your actual journal, fancied up."

Rosalind nodded. "I journal while events are fresh in my mind and don't have the possibility of being corrupted by other influences or by discussing what happened. If the discussions come across to me as meaningful, I'll write those up later."

"You were hiding this information in a frothy over-written romance novel?" Devin asked, one eyebrow indicating disbelief.

"Written within the genre, which allows me to spend more time in detailed descriptions and noting how people react to situations than my other work." Even to her ears, she sounded defensive. "Sorry, I can get like a mama bear with my work, especially when it's still in the toddler stage."

"It was brilliant!" Sydney reached out to grasp Roz's hand. "If anyone would come across a copy, they'd glance through it, see the prose and descriptions, the tag lines on the conversation, and blow it off. Setting it a hundred years ago was icing on the cake."

Rosalind allowed herself a slight smile and relaxed her neck. "That was kind of the idea, but thanks for noticing. Actually, when the trouble started I thought the journal was what they were after, since it does describe Hamad's family problems and how he was forced to live a false life to please them."

"You thought they'd do anything to protect the family name?"

"Pretty much. Then Hamad died. Or I thought he did. Maybe he did and they're doing some kind of convoluted cover up. It's hard to say. But until I heard he was alive, with his family, ready to marry the cousin he swore he despised, I was sure he was a poor misunderstood young man, maybe confused about his sexuality, and needing a friend."

"And since you were so used to helping young men in that situation…" Ty reached for the coffee carafe.

"It never occurred to me he could be anything else. Idiot."

Ty cupped his hand over her knotted fingers and eased the strain. She looked over at him, expecting an uplifting support. Instead, she got, "Yeah, but you meant it in the nicest way."

"Asshole." She snorted, then her shoulders shook with suppressed laughter. She pulled her hands out from under his and tried to push him off the chair or at least away from her side where she felt his heat from shoulder to elbow. "Might as well be trying to move a mountain."

Devin smirked. "Since his head is ninety percent granite, you're not far off there."

"As if you're Mr. Warm and Fuzzy and Supportive?" Sydney asked, while watching her computer run another search.

"For certain people, I can be real warm and fuzzy.

Didn't hear any complaints last—" Devin's words were cut off by a small hand with long fingernails, over his mouth. His eyes danced above the brightly painted nails.

"With that out of the way." Rosalind pulled a yellow pad closer, picked up a pen. "What did you find you thought might be significant?"

They settled down for a serious discussion.

"I was seeing quite a few references to slavery, to oppression, and to the leaders of the Southern army. Some in defense, and some in disagreement. Was that factual or embellishment?"

"Factual. Raheem and a couple of his buddies would start discussing American history. Some of them said they were looking for details they couldn't find in the books, even when they went to college in the US. They knew I was a writer, who did a wealth of research in many different directions, so they would corner me and pump me for finer points and technicalities."

She hesitated, going over details in her mind as she searched her memory. "I didn't catch it at the time, since they would also ask about American music, like jazz and hip hop, but many of their questions had to do with African Americans and persons of color, with their history in the US and how they'd been oppressed. Along with their contribution to American history and culture, for which they got little credit."

She groaned, looked up at the ceiling. "They would always bring up the suffragettes, the fight for women's vote, and awful fashions. Which would distract me, because their anti-women messages and attitudes drove me nuts. They acted as if the suffragettes should never have been allowed to act that way. Especially when they complained about American fashions while trying to look down my dress, with three fingers of exclusive single malt in their glass tumblers."

Ty's narrowed eyes promised retribution. "Assholes."

"That's pretty much the worst thing you can call them. You can get a rise out of them, when you compare them to an animal, particularly the dirty regions. I teased one of them about being a jackass and he nearly took my head off."

Sydney nodded, pouring hot water into a tea pot. "I saw that reference. Pretty scary stuff."

"Fortunately, for me, Hamad's friends gathered around. At the time, I thought they meant to defend me, but now I'm thinking they worked too long to get me there, to set me up, and didn't want to lose whatever plan they had in play if he tried to break my neck or at least hurt me enough I would decide to leave." She snorted, reaching for her coffee mug. "At the time, I was grateful to them."

"With these references to oppression, to the Civil War leaders, and to what they see as taking advantage of the black man, I'm thinking the Stone Mountain reference has greater significance. Especially given Tony's history with the area," Sydney mused, reaching for her cooling tea.

"What's the date?" Ty asked abruptly then glanced at his watch.

"November ninth. Why?"

"November eleventh ring a bell with any of you?"

"November eleventh at eleven in the morning. Eleventh hour of the eleventh day of the eleventh month. Armistice Day, when the guns on the Western Front of the first World War went silent, signaling the end of the most horrific war most of the world had ever seen."

"Who would have known it was a forerunner to much worse?" Ty's voice was somber.

Roz sighed. "It signaled the end of innocence for most of its participants. The link between historic 'manly' wars and modern impersonal warfare. Pretty hard to write paeans to cream-of-man soup."

"Yuck, Roz. Where did that come from?"

"That's what happens when a mortar goes off in the trenches filled with rain water and desperate men."

"Does your research ever give you nightmares?"

"Perpetually. That's why I write it up and move on. Most of the time, anyway. I also have the idiotic notion if enough people write about this nonsense, and enough people read what we write, maybe it won't happen again."

"So you do understand why I keep working with Powers." Sydney sounded almost relieved.

"More than you might know. At least I understand your intent. Working with him, on the other hand—"

"He's not always as bad as he's been with you."

"He's also not big on support and understanding."

"That's true, but he has a lot on his plate."

"Not a lot of room for support and understanding when your plate is full of mistrust and manipulation," Ty pointed out. "I wouldn't put it past him to threaten Roz with some kind of exposure if he wanted or needed something from her."

"Possible. But he does learn from his mistakes. It's even possible that, in the future, he'll ask first and threaten later."

"We can only hope."

"It's not like he scares me." At the sight of two sets of lifted male eyebrows, Rosalind shrugged. "Okay, he scares me, but a lot of things have scared me more and I've gotten past them. Thing is, will he listen to what we have to say about the possible threat?" When their blank stares made it obvious they had lost the thread, she added, "Veterans' Day at Stone Mountain?"

"Taking all the evidence into account, it seems like the most logical possibility." Sydney reached for her phone. "Let's give the old fart a call."

❧❧❧

Powers's expression held little welcome. "This is an interesting supposition but not one we haven't considered. Though it would have been nice to have the additional data before."

"Yeah, well it would have been nice if you had come up with her computer before she had to threaten you," Ty pointed out.

This time he stood behind Roz's chair in support, glaring at the bodyguards behind Powers.

"No need to be testy, Mr. Randolph. We're all on the same side here."

"Sometimes I wonder what side that might be, considering you live in a circle of mistrust," Devin muttered while reaching for the coffee carafe.

"Well put, but not significant at this time. Be that as it may, we have been in discussion with the Georgia State Police, CID, and they have reviewed security at several potential sites. Including Stone Mountain."

"And what have they found?" Rosalind asked.

"Nothing obvious, no sign of any infiltration, no strange characters on the videos. Recent hires, within the last six months, are all locals with long-time ties to the community." He gave them all a smug smile. "These people know their jobs."

"'These people,'" Rosalind pointed out in a low, dangerous voice, "were aware of, and unwilling to prosecute, gross misconduct under the power of authority when their own locals with long-time ties to the community beat the crap out of Anthony Waters, tossed him over a cliff to die, and sodomized his lover with their night sticks, leaving his mangled body in the woods. Sorry if I don't have the same feelings of love and camaraderie you seem to feel, Major Powers."

She sat straight, eyes glittering like hard jewels. Catching her in the reflection from the mirror across the room, Ty could see the barbarian warrior queen Tony brought out for his artwork and could better understand her determination.

Powers cleared his throat, looked at the papers in front of him, then looked back up. "An unfortunate situation. Even tragic. But one which could, and probably does, have significance relating to what we are attempting to uncover now."

"Granted. So tell me, Major Powers." Rosalind nodded. "Now that we're all cooperating and communicating so well. Have you located Tony Waters?"

"Not at this time, no."

"Have you done a check of morgues and hospitals?"

"This isn't our first investigation, Ms. Summerton."

"It's not my first one either, Major Powers. And you didn't answer my question."

He cleared his throat again. "We have made that request of local officials."

"You didn't do it yourself?" Rosalind stilled, as if trying to push away the stress in her voice.

"We do not have unlimited manpower, and we cannot interfere in local law enforcement without their request."

"Guess what? Not being a part of this elite, highly-trained group of yours, I can." She rose, and flashed a wide smile when Sydney rose with her.

"For the duration and given your emotional attachment, I'm putting you on leave." Powers indicated Devin and Sydney in this statement.

They nodded.

❦❦

"Did you notice," Devin began as they headed toward the elevator, "how he looked awful damned pleased with himself?"

"Manipulative bastard probably thought he was herding us this way from the beginning," Ty growled.

"Not realizing he'd met his match in our tall friend here." Sydney nodded at Rosalind as they entered the elevator. "When did you figure out he would jump this way?"

"Guessed more than figured. It's obvious he doesn't like going through locals, but he wants resolution and knows he might need cooperation in the future. I think he recognizes there's an injustice here he can't resolve on his own. I read him as manipulative, with an eye on the goal, but not at all fond of people trying to block or manipulate him."

"Got it in one," Sydney agreed.

Ty angled his head to look over at Roz. "Damn, you are one smart woman. Do you know how sexy that is?"

Roz snorted inelegantly. "For someone as horny as you are, Ty, a loose thread on a denim jacket is sexy."

"You never know what you can get if you pull that thread." But his eyes never left hers, and he started to back her into the corner of the elevator.

"Ahem, not alone here, buddy, and we have a job to do," Devin observed then turned to Rosalind. "He gets like this sometimes in the middle of an operation. You just have to knee him in the balls a couple of times, push his brain back up where it can be of some use."

"Since I might have some use for that part of his anatomy, I'll point out that he doesn't want to start something we can't finish in the here and now," Rosalind said mildly.

The door whooshed open at the underground garage. Ty's eyes promised retribution as he stepped out ahead of her. "Your day will come," he whispered, keeping her behind him.

"Promises, promises." She waited with Sydney until they gave the all clear, then headed toward the parked cars. A nod from one of the men hidden in a corner brought acknowledgment from Ty and Devin, but they still inspected their vehicles before standing back to click open the doors.

Rosalind looked around at the sparsely occupied parking. "So, where do we start first?"

"I've done what I can hacking into the local data bases," Sydney began. "Started it this morning before we came over. It seemed like Powers would try something like this. I've worked with him for a while now and sometimes even I can figure out what's going on in that maze he calls a mind."

"Frightening thought."

"You know it. Anyway, as of this morning, no unidentified African American males of Tony's height and weight have arrived in the morgues. At least not that they've entered in the register. And of course no one with his name."

"That's something anyway." Roz sagged with relief, before she straightened her spine and nodded in thanks. "Hard to say what color his hair will be today. He wears it longer and usually straight. Not sure how we'll cover all the hospitals."

"I also checked into police reports. Got a few possible hits there. If we can get out to where I can have better reception I can check up on them."

"You're a little bit scary sometimes. You hacked into the police data banks?" Ty's voice seemed serious though his eyes sparkled.

"Ought to see her sneak into Homeland Security," Devin muttered. "I think it turns her on more than just about anything else."

"Except you, big guy. Don't let it crush your ego."

They piled into the two vehicles and eased out of the parking lot, looking both ways, then up, down, and across the street before emerging into the light.

Chapter 13

It took a few more hours, but finally they tracked down several possibilities and, by noon, Rosalind was easing around the door of a room in a small hospital. The nurse had left the room, with an admonition for the patient to "Just rest now." Which meant, Rosalind hoped, that the doctor had already been by and no one would disturb them. At first it was hard to tell, with bandages covering most of his face, but she saw something in the shape of the swollen fingers to let her know it was Tony, and she slipped into the room.

His breathing was labored, even with the boost of the oxygen through the cannula inserted under his nose. A metal stand held bags of medicine leading to the tube inserted into his arms, while another tube snaked out from under the sheet, with blood traces in the lower bag. The bruising under his fine mahogany skin turned it even darker, with purple undertones. His mouth was swollen and split, and someone had ripped the gold earring from his ear.

Swallowing back her tears and rage, she laid her hand gently on his arm, gave it a tiny shake. "Tony? Hey, hot stuff, you in there?"

His heavy curved lashes lifted, revealing dark eyes foggy with pain and drugs. "Roz?" he mouthed then swiped his tongue over his lips.

Seeing the cup and straw, Rosalind held it up to his battered mouth.

He sipped carefully. "Damn, girl, how'd you get here?"

"Plane, car, truck, bomb. You name it, I've been through it lately."

"Tried to warn you."

"Florida? You could have left something a little less cryptic. Or do you mean the Stone Mountain web site?" At his nod, she went on crisply. "Talk about cryptic. Did you think I brought my magic decoder ring with me?"

"Funny girl." He shifted then grimaced and lay still. "God, Roz, I am so sorry I got you into this."

With that, many of her hopes crashed and burned. After a minute to compose herself, she trudged on. "We can get into that later. For right now, you're going to have to suck it up and fill me in on what exactly 'this' is."

"Why don't you give him what we figured out, and let him agree or not?" Ty's voice rumbled from behind her, and she felt his welcome warmth at her back. "That way I'll know how much more I'll have to beat the crap out of him once he's out of this hospital."

Tony winced, as his nod brought more pain.

"Where to start," Roz mumbled. "Okay, you introduced me to Hamad. Did you know at the time he and his friends were looking for a patsy to use as a cover for their terrorist plans?"

Tony's eyes widened, and he attempted to shake his head frantically. Tears oozed from the corners of his eyes.

"Best not try that again. We can't have you fainting before we get our answers," Ty warned, almost sounding sympathetic.

"No," Tony managed to croak. "I introduced you, thought it would be that opportunity to see the Middle East from an insider's point of view you were looking for. I knew Hamad was one of us, but didn't know his friends were terrorists, much less him. He said something about how it would be great if his mother thought he'd found a woman, even if she was an American." He took another tiny sip of the water from the cup Rosalind held. "I'm pretty sure he saw us around the show before we met."

"Did you meet Raheem before you met Hamad?"

"I didn't meet Raheem at all until I landed in Atlanta." His eyes still held hers without flinching.

"Did you know what they were planning here in Georgia?"

Now he did flinched and tried to look away.

Ty's hand came around her, holding the much smaller man's chin so he couldn't turn his head. "You want to keep your head on your neck, you'd better answer honest and fast."

"I didn't know right away. Talked to Hamad during the horse show. Guy things mostly. Okay, gay guy things. And some about being a gay, black guy in this country, even now. I might have—" He stopped and self-corrected. "—probably did tell him about never wanting to be in Georgia again, about that song 'Night the Lights went out in Georgia.' The whole big-bellied sheriff thing. You know, we've talked about it before."

"I wonder if that's why he asked me about it. I thought you'd gotten past that."

"Therapy can only do so much. There are some memories you never lose, some you really don't want to lose."

This time when he turned his face away and closed his eyes, they let him.

After a minute, and another swallow of water, he went on. "They called me a while after you arrived. Told me you'd disappeared. I think they tried to tell me you went off the deep end but gave it up pretty fast when I refused to believe them. Just said you went off on a night ride and hadn't returned. I couldn't get clearance to go there."

"Nobody could," Ty pointed out. "They put a lock down on the country. A subtle one by losing paperwork and not returning phone calls."

"Right. Then I remembered a friend of a friend. Someone I met at one of the special parties."

She nodded, understanding. Tony was talking about the private parties between gay men in sensitive jobs, who were so far into the closet they were simply rearranging the shelves.

"One of them was telling me about a shadow group that could get things done when even the SEALs couldn't. I gave him a call and laid it all out for him. He said he'd do what he could, and he did."

"That just saved your life," Ty said. This time the nod was minuscule but the relief was obvious. "So your call to New Mexico?" Ty continued.

"The shoot was legit, I had contracts to fill. I had to see you face to face, to be sure you were okay. You weren't answering your phone in New York when I knew you were back and out of the hospital. I went by your place. Your neighbor said you left the day before. Finally got your agent to tell me where you were and give me your new number."

"I changed my cell phone number and carrier when I got back. Too many people I didn't want to talk to knew the old one—"

"Enough old time's sake," Ty broke in. "And you'd best believe you're going to come up with the whole story sooner rather than later. For now, what's the plan and who put you in the hospital?"

Tony's dull eyes went past them to the door and widened in shock. Ty turned smoothly, reaching behind his back, under his jacket.

"You're lucky it was us, old man. You're slipping," Devin whispered as he and Sydney eased into the room. He closed the door and leaned against it. "This the asshole?"

Rosalind nodded and forcibly pushed her heart back into her chest from where she'd felt it jump into her throat.

"He know what's going down?"

Tony gave a tiny nod then closed his eyes.

"Stay with me, Tony, dammit," Rosalind urged.

His eyes opened again slowly. "I'm not leaving yet."

"You need the nurse?"

"No, I hurt enough already. Water." Another sip, and he forged on in his painful whisper of a voice. "How'd you find me?"

"I started calling hospitals with a delivery for Jason Antoine." For the sake of the others, she added, "It's a name he used for some art shows, especially when his hair was blond."

"Stupid name, but sometimes I gotta flame."

"I think the morphine might have kicked in." She

tapped an unbruised part of his cheek. "Come on, now's the time to come clean, be a hero, save the day, and convince us we can fast talk you out of jail time. Who beat the snot out of you?"

"When I learned about what they were really going to do instead of what they first told me, I went to Stone Mountain."

"Back up. First plan?"

"Demonstration. Desecrate the carvings with paint balls, put out signs about racism and a monument to an oppressive way of life. Make a point, strike a mark, all that blah, blah." His voice faded.

"I can see that appealing to you, but I can't believe you were stupid enough to believe that's all they intended to do."

"Color me stupid."

"It's better than that damned eggplant you tried to color me one time. Did you warn Stone Mountain?"

"Didn't get past the front desk. My old buddy was there and he remembered me."

"He did this to you? That lard-assed no-neck you ran into before?"

"No, he wouldn't let me past the front door to talk to someone with an actual measurable IQ."

Sydney, who had stepped away, returned and flipped her phone shut. "No one at Stone Mountain security has any record of a reported threat possibility."

Tony sighed, tried to squirm. Grimaced.

"Don't worry. They managed to hack into my server and my computer and wipe out the message you sent me. If it weren't for Ty and these guys—" She sent a grateful look at the three crowding in the room. "—no one would have believed you'd sent that message."

"Why?" he croaked

"At first, I was thinking they wanted to set me up to take the fall for whatever they're planning. Now I'm not so sure it isn't because they have someone who can hack, and they're doing it because they can."

"Pretty stupid reason to make that much effort," Ty observed.

"Just being from the Middle East and angry doesn't make them terrorist leaders. A lot of times, they come across as more like wanna-be gangies flashing their signs. Mostly teens or young twenties, not a lot of sense and none of it common. Trying to find their place in the world."

"Roz, you can't tell me you feel sorry for them?" Ty snapped out.

"Hell, no. Too many people in their country live a hand-to-mouth existence. They can barely read and have to share an oven with the rest of the community. They are essentially kept one step above the Stone Age by a society not far removed from the South in the early nineteenth century. Thing is, it's the twenty-first century now, and it's way past time they moved up to flush toilets and open elections."

Tony's hand slipped out from under the covers, found hers, squeezed lightly. A ghost of a smile pulled at his cracked lips. "My girl. They didn't know what they let themselves in for, messing with you."

"Their mistake was coming over here to our schools, learning about computers and technology, and ignoring the ethics classes. Our mistake is letting them only learn an overview of our history, most of it taught by apologists who don't know how good they have it. They sit up there in their ivory towers, throwing stones at the people who make it possible for them to criticize their government without fear."

They heard the sound of a pair of hands clapping outside the door. Devin stepped away, then opened the door partially to see Powers and his body guards, blocking the hallway. "Bravo, Ms. Summerton. We could find a position for you writing advertising copy."

"Sorry, I already have a job. One where I can look myself in the mirror every morning and sleep soundly at night."

"Your mistrust is understood but possibly misplaced. However, that is for a future discussion. For now—" He stepped into the room and eyed Tony, who looked back at him as defiantly as he could, given the level of pain and drugs in his body. "For now, we'd best get this man moved to somewhere more secure, under the care of a good doctor."

"The doctors here are fine." Tony managed to inject bravado into the statement.

"The security here is abysmal, and the fact that your attack didn't show up on any police reports is highly suspect. I'd rather get you moved and under our care before someone comes in to finish the job."

"Which reminds me." Sydney stepped between Tony and Powers. "Who did this to you?"

"Hamad's friend Raheem has some US friends, allies, whatever. They must have followed me from Stone Mountain. They jumped me at a rest area."

"Any chance they knew no-neck?"

"Wouldn't surprise me."

"Could you describe them well enough for identification?" Powers asked, earning himself a withering glare from Rosalind.

"Don't you people ever do any research? Put a pencil in his hand, he can draw them for you."

Powers scowled at her. "He's a photographer. I doubt he had time to take pictures."

"He's an artist. Try Googling Jason Antoine. He's done the covers for a lot of major fantasy authors and his posters are one of the best sellers at FF&P conventions."

Powers looked grim. It was obvious he was going to have a serious discussion with his research team.

"Bet you're really missing Syd these days," Devin taunted, earning himself an elbow in the ribs from his wife, followed by an intimate smile.

"You have no idea," Powers growled. "Ready out there?"

They heard a disturbance in the hallway, questions from someone concerning who they were and why they were there. An exhausted-looking young doctor pushed his way into the room. At a nod from Tony, Devin stepped out of the way.

"Who the hell are all of you? Are you nuts? This man can't be moved." Exhausted or not, the doctor was determined to protect Tony.

"What's the damage?" Rosalind drew up to her full height and gave him the undiluted effect of her lavender eyes.

He stared for a minute, then gulped, and fought for his dignity. "Massive internal injuries, numerous lacerations, potential skull fracture. Nearly crushed larynx. No idea how many ligaments are damaged in his arms and shoulders."

"Ouch. They hold your arms while someone else whaled on you?" Ty asked with a hint of sympathy. Tony nodded faintly. "Must of thought you were one hell of a threat, puny little guy like you."

This brought a small grin from Tony, and a sound of exasperation from the doctor. "Whoever the hell you are, you have to leave this room now before I call security."

The looks of comical disbelief were shared across all those watching him. Then the men behind Powers lifted their jackets to reveal their guns in shoulder holsters.

"We were just discussing the security in this hospital, as a matter of fact," Powers continued blandly. "If we had meant any harm to your patient, he would have been dead before you even knew we were on the floor." He looked over as one of his body guards signaled. "Very well. We have an ambulance ready to receive him in the under-ground lot. This is our gurney, and here is our transportation crew."

Medics moved through the door, pushing a well-padded gurney ahead of them. One of them said, "We're going to need some space here."

Powers looked at the group in the room. As one, they looked to Rosalind, who nodded reluctantly. "Yeah, I think we need to get him out of here," she said. "Can we have a copy of his medical charts and treatment?"

The doctor hesitated, clearly torn between his concern as a physician and the obvious truth he was in over his head. Then he nodded. "I'll have them for you before he leaves."

"A thought, Doctor...Mason, is it?" Powers peered at the name badge. Getting a nod, he went on. "Let's not show this room as empty. I have someone in mind who needs a bit of a rest. If you could possibly rent us the room, I doubt for too much longer? A camera here?" Something clicked behind them, taking detailed photos of the room. "Let's leave Mr. Waters some privacy. Could we possibly give him a fresh bag, so we can keep this bag here, to lend some authenticity?"

They filed out of the room, letting the medics in, along with a slender black agent who was loosening his tie as he came through the door.

"Okay, that was clever. Maybe you can go back to being one of the smartest men I've ever met. You still piss me off," Ty said as he leaned against the wall, casually watching down the hallway. Devin took up the same position, looking the other direction.

"Your approval being, of course, the main goal of my life." Powers conferred with his assistant then turned back. "And I can sympathize about upsetting you. This entire sequence of events hasn't left me feeling very charitable toward several of what should be our fellow agencies. Be that as it may," he continued, "at the moment, we need to move Mr. Waters to a place with stronger security and you need to move on before those agencies stop tripping over each other and find you here. This is not a good time for any of you to be showing up at police headquarters."

"Speaking of police, anyone cooperating there?" Sydney asked.

"Georgia CID is proving to be somewhat cooperative, though they have a problem with a 'vague potential threat to somewhere in Georgia at some time coming up soon.'"

They all hesitated when a muffled curse came from the room behind them. Rosalind took a step in that direction, but stopped when Powers held up his hand. "I've no doubt he was transferred to the other gurney and is now being settled for travel. Don't forget his doctor, who is not in my employ, is also in there."

The door swung open shortly after that to reveal Tony, his face gray against white sheets, being wheeled out while his doctor replaced bandages on the decoy.

"Makeup," Rosalind said, seemingly into thin air.

"Good point," Powers murmured, and gestured.

A man stepped forward, took out what looked like a paint swatch, held it up to Tony's face. He nodded and went into the room with a large bag.

"Finally get to work on your ugly self," they heard as the door closed.

Rosalind leaned over the gurney, Tony was gesturing weakly. "What's up, bonehead?"

"Not a lot of time," Tony whispered.

"How long?"

"Tomorrow. Light show, fireworks. Vet's day."

"Gates will be guarded," Ty reminded him.

"Probably already in there. Would have come in last night or with today's, yesterday's, crowd. Snipers. Paint guns for some, real guns for others. Some kind of explosion. They know about private back roads."

"I'm betting we're going to find lard-ass involved right up to his nonexistent neck," Rosalind growled.

Tony nodded weakly, patted her hand.

"Anything else we need to know right now, Mr. Waters?" Powers waited until Tony weakly shook his head, then he gestured at the support team. "Very well. We will keep you apprised of what occurs, and wait for your drawings. Your assistance has been invaluable."

The medical team pulled the sheet over his mouth so only the bandages showed, then wheeled him off down the hallway, chattering among themselves about scheduled surgeries and the cafeteria special.

"It's a good team. You can relax about your friend. He'll be in good hands."

They followed him down the hallway. Rosalind noticed the orderlies chatting at the end of the hallway near the doors to the stairway, then a young couple in the family waiting room, who seemed more involved watching the people in the hallway than in the television or magazines. Powers nodded without looking at them directly and they went into a new stage of alert while managing to look uninterested in anything but each other.

"I'm thinking there's going to be some action in that room pretty soon," Roz muttered.

"I'm thinking you might be right." Sydney turned to Powers as they filed into the elevator. "What's next?"

"First, we need to remove to another location, where we can talk without anyone eavesdropping. Then we need to bring in someone local, possibly from Stone Mountain."

"You don't think they've already been poisoned against any talk of terrorists by now?"

"Not everyone listens to someone who has been put

into a position because he can't be fired and is an embar-
rassment to the uniform."

∾∾

Which was exactly what they found to be the case
when they met with a keen-eyed representative from the
state police. This was not someone who would blow off a
complaint about an abuse of justice. He listened to what
they had learned from Tony and immediately pulled out
his phone, started to make calls.

Rosalind made no pretense of hiding her disgust. "So
where were you eight years ago? Or does it take the back-
ing of someone like Powers to get justice here?"

"I was driving patrol in Marietta eight years ago, but
you can best believe I heard about the gay bashing and
murder out near Stone Mountain. I'm ashamed to admit
some of my fellow officers weren't too sympathetic.
Some black men have a problem with the idea that anyone of color can be anything other than red blooded het-
erosexual." He extended his own dark hand, looked at it
for a minute, then met her eyes straight on. "I'm not one
of them. I figure what you do in your bedroom, or car, or
in the woods, is your own business as long as both of you
are of age and consenting."

He settled his gun on his hip, looked around. "Simple
as that. What was done to your friend and his lover has
left a stink in the nostrils of a lot of us, along with what

wasn't done to the perpetrators. Some of us have long memories, and some of us also keep our ears open. We have a different leadership than we had eight years ago, and I'd like to think we've learned a bit along the way." He looked around again, nodded. "I'm fixing to kick some terrorist butt. You guys wanna come along?"

"Don't even try to stop me," Sydney warned Devin.

He gulped. "Wasn't thinking of it."

Roz hesitated. "I don't know about you guys, but I'm not trained for this kind of action. I would, however, very much appreciate being somewhere I could observe. Maybe I could have someone with me to interpret what's happening, identify weapons, that kind of thing?"

Sydney glared at her. "Like I can't recognize that as trying to get me out of harm's way? Fine, I'll play your silly little game."

Devin sent Roz a look of heartfelt thanks.

Chapter 14

You think they're going to stay out of trouble up there?" Ty asked Devin in an undertone later as they followed the local cops up a secret trail through the woods surrounding Stone Mountain.

"I think Rosalind will do everything she can to protect Sydney, and vice versa. Seems like they see each other as the sister they didn't have."

"Let's hope. It'll help to have Roz around later to identify the assholes."

༼༽

"You really think I pulled you up here to keep you safe?" Rosalind asked, checking out the view from the observation post. Below, paths and rough roads meandered among the dark, thick trees. Lights showed closer to the large stone edifice.

Sydney snorted. "Pretty damned obvious from where I sat. I'm not helpless because I'm pregnant, any more than you're stupid because you're so damned gorgeous."

"I've seen you in action. You're far from helpless. You can probably knock your Neanderthal of a husband on his butt."

"Five times out of six, but I really don't play fair."

They shared an intimate grin.

"The thing is, I really am way out of my element here, and I found out damned fast in the Middle East that doesn't do anyone any good. I know this is your milieu, to use one of Tony's words, and hope you can help me stay sane by feeding me details I'd miss."

Sydney nodded then grinned. "You plan to use this in a book?"

"You bet your pint-sized ass I do. There's a lot more inside my head than books for younger people who need quality guidance." Rosalind ran a hand over her short strands and winced. "And doesn't that sound pompous?" She shifted, moving closer to one of the windows overlooking the back of the park.

"I've been hiding in my books, same way as I have in my life. It's a mistake going for the safe and known, instead of taking a chance on the new. That's why the trip to the Middle East was such a temptation. Sure, I've traveled before, but generally as part of a fashion shoot along with other models. I could arrange my own transportation, book a flight or a car, no problem. But I didn't stray far from work."

"Bet they loved having you on assignment."

"Bet you're right. I was the one person they were sure they wouldn't find dragging a strange man or woman to the set. Or be discovered passed out in their room when they didn't show up for a shoot. They considered me the consummate professional, when actually I was the complete coward."

Sydney gave her the one eyebrow look. "Kind of hard on yourself there."

"If I didn't look too far beyond the barricade, I couldn't get hurt. My mom wasn't like that. She always lived life full out. Give her a mascara wand, dark red lipstick, and some high heeled boots, and she was up for pretty much anything. Or any one."

"Did you resent that?"

Rosalind turned to face the other woman. "Shrink much, Sydney? Nah, I loved her, eventually realized we're not the same person. Since she realized the same thing, we got along pretty darned well most of the time. She never completely understood me giving up the glamor and big paychecks of modeling to write books that might or might not sell, but she bragged on me to all her friends and pushed them to buy my books as gifts for their kids."

"Can't do much better than that." Sydney looked out the observation window of the ranger's station then listened to the low voiced comments coming through her earpiece. "Okay, grab your glasses. Look down there to your left." She grabbed her own small, powerful binoculars.

Rosalind raised the field glasses to her eyes and focused. The blur sharpened into separate people, some in uniform, some not, moving forward at a crouch.

Next to her, Sydney said, "The light show's scheduled to start any time now, and it's most probable they planned to use that as a starting point for their attack. It would offer maximum confusion and the best opportunity to get away." She studied the scene then turned to Rosalind. "Some nice weapons down there, but I'm not sure these guys know how to use them. That's a Sharps with a fancy scope, really more suited to long range work than up close and personal. Those three hunters over to the east?"

She looked over to be sure Rosalind's binoculars pointed in the same direction. "There's your good ol' boys with their deer rifles. 'Officer, I know my rights. Constitushun says I can carry a gun.'" Sydney drawled this in an exaggerated mumble, then changed to a Southern accent but in a crisp voice, sharp with authority. "Second Amendment calls for a well-armed militia, not for a bunch of bozos to try to shoot up a Vets' Day celebration."

Rosalind choked back a giggle then let out a full-bellied laugh. "You're good at that."

"Knowing what they're probably saying? I've had to deal with the bozos of the world for years."

Rosalind took notes between peering at the action outside. With Sydney's direction, prompted by more discussion over the headset, she watched another group being taken down, this time assisted by two large men in dark clothing who moved over the ground like phantoms. She had no problems recognizing Ty's familiar lean form. "They've done this before, I take it?"

"Oh, yeah. They were doing this years ago, long before Ty settled down on the family ranch. Devin followed his example a couple years later."

"You too?"

Sydney turned to face Rosalind. "This was more of the family business for me. My dad spent of most of his life as a free-lance soldier and it seemed perfectly natural for me to go along with him. Lana, my sister—Ty's former wife?—she stayed with our mom. It actually worked out pretty well for me. I know how to field strip most weapons, got a great background in coordinating missions and field ops. I learned computers in the field which gave me a leg up on people who only knew programming, not practical application."

"You do realize you're going to have to go in a book some day?"

"If you write about me, can you make me a couple of

inches taller?" Sydney injected a bit of whine into her rich alto voice. "I've always wanted to be tall enough for people to have some respect for me. Not as tall as you, you're just freakishly tall."

Rosalind shrugged, then took a deep breath. "Sydney…" She blew out the breath. "Why are you being so nice to me?"

Sydney scowled. "Why not? I thought we were friends."

"I hope so, but you helping me like this seems to go above and beyond friendship."

Sydney's expression grew somber. "We'd do it for Ty anyway. He's more than family. He'd do it for us. But this…" Sydney swept out her hand, encompassing Rosalind and the activity outside. "This is for you. The first time I met you seemed like I'd known you before."

"Sisters from different mothers?" Rosalind suggested. "Same for me, but it seemed too…romantic to say anything."

"There's more to friendship, and love, than just romance."

"There's no such thing as 'just' romance!" Rosalind insisted, then smiled

"True. But what's between you and Ty? That's way beyond romance. You make him happy, and he so deserves to be happy."

"I drive him nuts."

"Absolutely. That's part of what makes him happy."

They stared at each other then stepped forward into a strong hug. And stepped back, not hiding how they needed to wipe at their cheeks.

Sydney reached for her backpack. "Looks like it's about time to pack it in and see what we can con those men into buying us for dinner." She hefted the bag on her back "I, for one, could eat the rear half of a cow that's had vodka rubbed into its hide for about a year."

"Yummm Kobe beef. Good stuff and to heck with our arteries. Are we supposed to wait here or meet them somewhere?"

Sydney keyed her earbud to ask, listen, and agree. "Looks like they got everyone playing soldier they could find. They want us to meet them down below. They can identify quite a few of the faces from your pictures, and Tony's drawings, but aren't sure on others. Makes it hard to know who isn't there. Of course, they're refusing to speak English so our guys are waiting for an interpreter."

"Devin's actually going to let you go down these dangerous, fully lit concrete stairs all by yourself?" Rosalind teased as they started down the steps.

Sydney flashed a lighthearted grin. "Wonders will never cease. I'm sure by the time we make that last turn, he'll be waiting at the bottom. And I'm betting his partner will be with him. Now that we have a minute, I wanted to ask you—"

"You're not going to have a chance to ask," a heavily accented voice came out of the dark, before a hand rose and fell, wielding a police baton. Sydney ducked. The baton landed on her shoulder instead of her head.

When she fell to the ground soundlessly, Rosalind could only gape. Instinct kicked in and she drew in a breath to scream.

"I don't think so. Welcome back, Rozzie."

Before a sound could escape a cloth covered her face, hard hands forcing her to breathe in rank fumes. Solid arms wrapped around her, trapping her arms against her body, leaving her well and truly trapped. She tried to kick out, but caught between her attacker and the narrow confines of the walkway, it was futile. Unable to fight the insidious darkness clamoring closer, she succumbed.

ಊಸಿ

Devin peered up the concrete steps, waiting impatiently for his wife to emerge. No doubt she was going to give him grief about him hovering. But marriage made a man think differently about things, and the responsibility grew exponentially at the idea of being a father.

"Settle down there. You act like you got ants in your pants. Geesh, give her some time to get packed up," Ty teased, while looking into the shadows below the observation station.

"Syd's always packed. Pain in the ass to be on a job with her, she's so damned efficient she makes everyone else look bad."

"Roz isn't. She's always looking around, grabbing one more thing to put in that giant satchel she carries."

Devin turned away from his intent perusal to tease. "You are so gone on her. I can see those little tweetie birds flying out of your mouth every time you say her name."

"You're thinking about yourself, bonehead."

"I don't think so. For me, it's more like butterflies. You always did make more noise than I did." He paused, eyeing his friend seriously. "Whatever it is, feels pretty damned good, doesn't it?"

Ty looked over, staying silent for a moment, before finally giving a quick nod. "Finding the one? You're damned right it does." He looked back up the steps, his lips curved in a smile, then he stiffened. "Something's wrong."

"Now who's the old woman?" Devin groused, but he was straightening from his casual lean as he picked up on Ty's tension.

"A rock came down from that dark area around the corner where the steps swoop down from the guard house."

Not waiting for anything more, they pounded up the steps, taking them two, three at a time. When they came around the corner, they saw minor signs of a scuffle, barely there marks disturbing the ground most people would ignore. For them, it was a fully lit billboard.

Ty dropped to his knees and lifted a brightly colored

flat heeled shoe from the dirt, next to Sydney's back pack. He drew in a breath, pulling himself together. Digging deep for the warrior he'd learned to be.

Devin pulled out his phone, and keyed in the emergency code. "Red alert, full lock down all exits."

A door slammed below them, on the dark road past the station. Feet pounded on the steps behind them, the emergency team coming to help. Ty pulled out a small flashlight and began to read the signs left on the ground. Find Rosalind. Then worry.

❧❧❧

Jostling under her body woke Rosalind, along with a headache of immense proportions. Around her, cursing in several languages emerged from the dark. Some of the languages sounded familiar, some didn't.

"You idiot. Why didn't you pull back the way we planned and slip out of the park? No muss, no fuss." That sounded like educated American.

"We're fine," another voice, accented and somehow familiar, answered.

"No, we would have *been* fine, but you had to grab both women and screw the plan. You think they won't stage a full scale search for them?" The first speaker was pissed, if the anger in his voice was anything to go by.

"It don't matter." A new voice, heavy on the Southern and she'd bet of the no-neck variety.

"Doesn't it? The teams grabbed the others, like we planned. If those two hadn't gone off on their own, the teams would never know any differently and would be happy with their catch. By the time the place went up, we would be scot free. Now, though—"

"They won't find us, not with our friend here's knowledge of these roads," said one of the accented voices from behind her. "Unless, of course, he doesn't know them the way he says he does."

"I know these roads just fine. Used to pot deer out here, off season." The heavy drawl identified the driver's no-neck status.

Rosalind took stock of her situation. Her hands were secured behind her back by something narrow, probably cable ties. Her shoulders screamed in protest of the unnatural position. More of the cable ties wrapped around her ankles. Under her shoulder she could feel the cool metal of the uncarpeted floor. Hard to miss as they hit another pothole and she bounced. Hard. But there was room wherever she was, which meant they were probably in a panel van. Another bruising jolt and bounce as they sped down a bad road. None of this helped the existing bruises.

Inching her eyes open, she found Sydney curled into a heap against the back of the passenger seat. For a moment her heart stopped, until she caught the subtle lift and close of Syd's eye in a deliberate wink. From her position and the uneven light she couldn't tell if they'd trussed

Sydney up like a chicken ready for grilling. When her vision wavered, she knew she was still suffering from whatever they used to put her under. She tried to brace herself unobtrusively, then froze as a voice spoke above her.

"The tall one is awake, Raheem." A heavy foot shoved her hip, moving her onto her back. Her shoulders protested the move, and the bouncing of the vehicle slammed the back of her head against the unforgiving floor.

Determined not to flinch, she stared up into a barely recognizable face above her. From the corner of her eye she saw the driver turn his head and glare at the group in the back of the van before bringing his attention back to the road. Tilting her head, she narrowed her eyes, trying to make out the man leaning over her. "Mansur?"

"That's right, bitch. Mansur. You didn't have time to talk to me in my country, now you will have plenty of time."

Before she could respond, the other idiot in the passenger seat said, "Not all that much time. I tell you, we have to dump the women and get out of here."

Mansur's lip curled as his contemptuous gaze flicked to Sydney, then back to the driver. "Dump the short one, she's no real use to me." He turned his malicious attention back to Rosalind. "I have unfinished business with this one."

"Dump both of them. Dammit, they're on the team.

As long as you have either one, the others won't give up." The passenger was Mr. Educated Voice.

Rosalind twisted her head to see the person in the passenger seat. She didn't recognize him at first but something struck her as though he might look familiar. Then she placed him. Stunned, she wondered why one of Powers's men would turn traitor

"I wouldn't recommend it, Carter." Sydney's voice came out of the dark corner where she braced herself. "You hurt one hair on her head, your life wouldn't be worth the powder it would take to blow you straight to hell." She rose to a more comfortable sitting position. "When your partners here grabbed us, you pretty much signed your death warrant. You know how Powers feels about traitors."

"I know how Powers feels about a lot of things. Like looking like a fool when he's trying to play lord high and mighty with the locals."

"So you were the one who messed up all the re-search?" Sydney shook her head and sighed. "What did you think it was going to get you? Once you screw over Powers, there's no hole on Earth big enough for you to crawl into and hide."

"I won't need to hide. I've been with Powers for long enough, I figured out how his mind works. I thought I'd gotten rid of you before when you lost your nerve and shacked up with that big cowboy. But you had to come back and try to show me up, acting like you know it all."

"Damn, Carter, I had no idea you were such a wee-nie." Her voice held scornful disbelief. "You kept this bottled up all this time? Why not quit and go with another group?"

"I worked my way up to the top with Powers. I'm not quitting just because he has the hots for some scrawny chick and gives her all the plum assignments." His voice rose with every sentence until he was nearly shouting.

Syd snorted. "You're even more delusional than I thought. I worked my butt off to earn Powers's respect. Those assignments were based on merit. Not who I might be screwing or who I could screw over at the water cool-er."

He shifted, coming up on a knee in his seat to reach over the back, groping for her hair. It was clearly what Syd needed, because he had no idea how close she was to the top of his seat. She straightened in a rush and jammed her skull into his nose, her shorter frame an advantage in the enclosed space. He screamed and grabbed his face, before falling over sideways into the driver. As the van started weaving, Rosalind drew her legs up, then jammed them into Mansur's stomach, pushing him against Ra-heem Both of them fell against the van window, then forward when the van swerved across the road, then tilted and came to an abrupt stop in a steep slant. Windshield glass crunched as both driver and passenger were pro-pelled forward.

Rosalind slid, ending up in a heap against the seats, with Sydney next to her.

"Oof. You damned giraffe, get off me," Sydney grunted.

"Gladly." Rosalind managed to shift her weight off the smaller woman. "Can you reach the side door?"

"Seeing as it's downhill, maybe. Hold on."

As Rosalind pulled back, Sydney edged out from under her, then slid down to the door. She tried pushing the handle with her elbow, and ended up maneuvering around to grab the handle with her bound hands.

"Glad we practiced crap like this at Dad's training camp." While she concentrated on what was behind her, she looked to the back of the van. "What's up with that a-hole who had his oversized sandals on your stomach?"

Rosalind cursed herself for losing track of the kidnappers stuck in the van with them. Mansur was sprawled out uncomfortably across the seat he'd occupied behind her, his back at an unnatural angle. It looked like Raheem's head had hit the van side forcefully enough to knock him out.

"Doesn't look like they'll be moving any time soon." She swallowed down the bile threatening to rise.

"Let's not give them an opportunity." The door clicked, then fell open. Sydney pushed forward to avoid tumbling out of the opening. She waited for any reaction, any sound, then peered out. "Looks clear. Let's go."

"Ummm, slight problem? Bound feet?"

"Take small steps. Move it, in case they have back up, or the windshield didn't do its job. We have to get to a phone or something and get word to the team about the explosives."

"You don't think they found everything?"

"Not leaving anything to chance is how we stay alive one more day."

"In that case." Rosalind scooted along on her butt to the door. There were times when long legs did more than get in your way. "I see my purse up in the corner behind where you were sitting." As she approached the door, she turned and grabbed the bag with her bound hands, then eased her legs out of the door, then hesitated, dropping the purse. "Might have a problem here, Syd. Can't feel my feet."

There was no sympathy to be found. "They're right there at the end of your legs. If your legs weren't so asininely long, you'd be able to feel them. Think about wiggling your toes."

After a minute of concentration Rosalind felt the slightest movement at the end of her legs. Trusting Sydney, she slid out the door and braced against the side of the van. "Ow…ow…ow. Pins and needles, and dammit I swear that was a knife in my ankle."

"Oh, shit," Sydney muttered, shuffling close. "Hold on, let me look. Crap." She straightened. "I don't see a knife, but I'm not seeing real clearly. Might be broken."

"Yeah, I kind of figured that, the way it didn't hold

much weight." Rosalind eased down the side of the van, fighting to keep from blacking out. "Can't figure out what hurts worse, shoulders or ankles."

"It won't hurt much longer if we don't get away from here. Those guys up front are starting to move around." While she talked, Sydney lowered to the ground and started squirming until she could get her arms under her rear and pull her legs through her linked hands.

"Hey, something you can do, I can do." Concentrating on a spot of clear sky between the trees and the rising moon, Rosalind curled, twisted, and contorted, then had her hands behind her thighs. With Sydney's help she got her legs through. "Did you chew off those cable ties?"

"Sharp edge on the side of the van. Over here." Sydney moved over to the twisted metal, and showed her where to rub the ties on a broken edge. Once their hands were free, they went to work on their ankles. Sydney picked a tiny knife out of the change pocket in her jeans and sawed industriously. "Here." She stuck her feet toward Rosalind's hands and carefully used the knife on the ropes at her feet. "You rub my feet, I'll get yours free."

The worked quietly for a few moments, before Sydney finally spoke, "Okay, good news. Probably not broken. Bad news, you actually do have some kind of metal thing in your ankle. I'm not too sure about pulling it out."

"The fun never ends around you. Since it's not broken, leave it." Rosalind tucked her feet under her butt, took hold of the van door, and rose carefully, then reached a hand down to Sydney. "Can you hand up my purse? I should have picked it up while I was down there. It's kind of far down now."

Giving her a mock glare, Sydney shuffled around. "No giggling. If you fall on me again, I'd be squashed flatter than a bug on a windshield."

"Before you get up, answer one question."

"Shoot, then I get to ask you one."

"How bad are your cramps?"

Silence from the huddled shape at her feet. "How the hell did you know when I barely knew?"

"You're working off adrenaline and used to ignoring pain to take command. I'm used to working in large groups of young women, some of whom still call their cycle 'the curse' or 'granny visiting.' I've been around too many women trying to hide cramps." She could see Sydney's upraised, pale face in the growing moon light.

"Cramps started when I woke up. Haven't gone away. Haven't gotten worse." Sydney looked around. "I don't see your purse."

"Oh. Oops. I didn't get it out of the van." She reached back in for the bag, and felt a hand clamp around her wrist.

"You thought you'd get away from me this easily, bitch?" Raheem's face loomed out of the dark van, blood pouring down from a gash over his eyes. "You ruined my lover's life, you won't survive to enjoy yours. After I kill you, I'll send your lover your hand in a box."

"No, asshole, you and your buddy over there ruined Hamad." She shook her head, disgusted. "God save us all from trite criminals. Couldn't you learn originality while you were in college?" She braced both feet on the ground and, ignoring the sharp bite of pain from her injured ankle, threw herself backward. Off balance and unprepared, Raheem sailed over her head and down the hill, hitting the ground, rolling, then crashing into a pine tree.

"Oops." Splayed on her back, Rosalind turned to her stomach and looked downhill. "Didn't really mean to do that. I only wanted to bring him out here so we could beat his brains out."

"We'd have to find them first." Sydney eased herself to her knees, dared a look into the van. "It doesn't look like anyone else will be moving any time soon." She grabbed at the bag, then sank back to the ground before she crawled over to Rosalind. "How you holding up?"

"I have a foreign object in my leg. I might have killed someone. My dearest friend is in her first trimester with trauma-induced cramps, and I think I broke a nail. Other than that, just dandy."

"Don't forget we still have to save the world, or at least that mob back at Stone Mountain." Sydney dug in the purse, coming up with various strange objects. "Where the hell is your phone?"

"Side pocket. Zipper. Pray it's not crushed."

"Not. Miracle. Battery's charged." Sydney frowned, then growled. "No damned signal. Why the hell can't it have a signal?" Her voice petered out in a whimper.

"'Cause life in general sucks." Rosalind rolled over, trying to keep her foot off the ground while she crawled around the side of the van. The ground shifted under her, she automatically dropped her foot down as a brace, and blacked out.

⚜

"So there the two of them were, half hysterical, banged up, giggling, and whining about no cell signal."

The familiar voice eased its way through the cotton in Rosalind's head. It was coming from somewhere above her, and she recognized the near-concrete pillow beneath her head as a hard thigh. She swallowed experimentally, clearing her throat. "Considering how close my hand is to a certain delicate part of your body, I think you might want to reconsider that last statement." She shifted, feeling deep cushioned seats and hearing the purr of a powerful engine.

The gentle fingers on her shoulder tightened then relaxed. "Thought that might get your attention. Easy, let Bob work on your ankle."

"You've got some stray stuff stuck in there," a new voice piped up. "I've sprayed it with pain killer and bug killer, then gave you a local shot of happy juice. I'll leave it to the real doctors to pull these pieces out, probably under anesthesia."

She licked her dry lips. "Sydney?"

"Up here," A soft voice came from the seat ahead. Roz eased her eyes open to dim lights. They were in a real van on plush seats. Since the luxurious bench seats faced each other, it might even be an SUV limousine, rushing them through the dark in ultimate comfort. Sydney was ensconced in Devin's arms, a blanket pulled over both of them.

Rosalind heard the pain in her friend's voice. "Why's she here? Why isn't she being airlifted out?"

"That rinky dinky cow path your kidnappers took is smack dab in the middle of the hills and heavy trees. Nowhere to land a chopper," Ty's voice rumbled above her head.

"But she's..." At a warning look from Sydney, Rosalind subsided.

"She's what?" Devin demanded

Sydney didn't give her a chance to answer. "Bruised and banged up and pissed off. I just had these nails done and now they're trashed."

"What about the explosives?" Rosalind grasped for a logical changed of subject.

"We took care of it. Couple of those losers we picked up were too willing to turn on their bosses, especially when they figured they been left holding the bag. They knew a lot more than the head guys thought, so they told us pretty much where they figured the big finale would be."

"In the grand scheme of things, they were pretty incompetent terrorists," Rosalind murmured.

Ty held her closer against his chest, and pulled the lightweight blanket up to her shoulders. "They still could have done some major damage if they'd managed to pull it all off."

"They would have without your help." Bob sat back from working on Roz's ankle. "You guys are real heroes."

Rosalind shook her head, easing her eyes open farther to address the medic. "The real heroes are the ones who get up every morning to put themselves in harm's way, never knowing if they're coming home at night. Me, I'm a writer. My big goal in life is to tell their stories."

Before anyone could respond, the SUV came out of the dark trees, into a meadow and an array of lights, some flashing. A helicopter sat off to one side, rotors turning slowly. Grim faced paramedics wrenched the doors open. "Who's hurt?"

"Tall one's got something in her leg, probably wrenched shoulders, and a real bad sense of humor," Devin said to their intense faces. "My wife here is three months pregnant and might be miscarrying." He looked down at her, his expression grim and worried. "You think I don't know every inch of your body, including how you breathe when you're hurt?"

He leaned forward and surrendered Sydney into their experienced hands, before getting out. A stretcher waited.

The EMTs set her down gently on a gurney then secured her at the thighs and ribs, before dropping a blanket over her.

The older EMT turned back to the others. "We've got another chopper on hold, coming in now. Meet you back at the hospital."

They rushed to the waiting chopper, Devin on their heels.

ɷɷ

Ty relinquished Rosalind to the next set of medics, her ankle supported by Bob until she was fully out of the SUV. They strapped her down, then dashed off to the second chopper.

Powers stopped Ty before he could follow. "Mr. Randolph, could you ride back into town with me? They'll give her an injection on the flight, or as soon as she's at the hospital, so she won't even know if you're there. We need to clear up a few matters."

Ty saw the group of men in black gathered on the road ahead of them and groaned.

Hearing his non-spoken question, Powers said, "No, we couldn't avoid them forever. We managed to hold them off long enough to air lift the women. They think the choppers will be going to Grady Memorial and plan to meet them there with armed guards. Most unfortunate. They didn't confirm the markings. You see, here come the agency choppers. The best you can do for Ms. Summerton now is to field their questions for a few hours."

Ty looked after the copter lifting off, his shoulders sagging. "But I don't know much beyond what's happened the last couple weeks, and damned little of that."

"Yes, most fortunate, wouldn't you say?" Powers smiled a very small, very private sort of smile.

ぐつぐつ

Rosalind woke to the sounds and smells that could only come from a hospital. She'd been in far too many critical care rooms not to recognize the hushed voices and beeping machines, or the moans from other cubicles. She let her eyes drift open. Curtains. Meant she was in post op.

Oh, yeah. Ankle. Surgery. Knife. Save the world. Sydney.

She sat bolt upright, or at least tried to. Her movements brought up the stranger in the chair next to her bed to their feet. They reached for her and scared the nurse who'd been checking her vital signs. "Ma'am, you need to lie down."

"Syd?" she whispered. She saw the head in front of her shake. She cried out and fell back against the pillows.

Ty came storming through the curtains. "What the hell happened?"

The guard stepped back. "She woke up, sat bolt upright on the bed, asked if my name was Sid. I tried to tell her no, but she passed out again."

"Moron." Ty forcibly pulled the young man out of the cubicle and pushed him into the hallway. "If you don't know the people on your team, you're useless to any of them. Move." He came to the head of the bed and leaned over to stroke her hair. "Roz? Come on, I know you're in there."

Two fat tears seeped out of her eyes and fell on the pillows.

"No, sweetheart, it's okay. Syd's fine. She's got Devin with her."

Her eyes opened slowly, bright with unshed tears, dull with pain. And drugs. "Baby?"

"Fine too. They'll want to keep her overnight and watch over her."

"Not lying to me?"

"Not lying. Swear to Mosby."

She managed a tiny smile then turned her head to nuzzle his palm. "Good. Glad you're here."

"Always will be."

About the Author

Mona Karel became convinced at an early age that her life would not really begin until she was about thirty-five. She has no idea what precipitated that thought, but she claims she was a strange child. Until reaching that age, she led a peripatetic existence for many years, criss-crossing the country, working with horses and dogs—and waiting tables to support her other jobs. At thirty-five, when many people are well into raising their families, Karel settled down to "real" work as a buyer and expediter. She married a high school teacher, which led to over twenty years in Southern California.

Karel can't remember a time she wasn't reading, though she doesn't remember much fun with Dick and Jane. Her preferred stories involved dogs and horses, and once she had gone through every horse book in the high school library, she started in on Civil War stories. They rode horses, didn't they? At that time Romance was swash-bucklers and Gothic. Karel preferred the stronger hero-ines and more subtle relationships of Mary Stewart, Helen MacInnes, and Andre Norton. Then Karel discovered Romance in the form of Silhouette, Candlelight, and RWA, and her life was complete. Karel has since retired to New Mexico, where she lives in the wind at 6,500 feet with her Salukis. When not writing or going to dog shows, Karel works at a solar-related firm.